P9-DDS-545

Charlie pulled up in front of the house and cut the engine, aware of Grace's gaze lingering on him.

He unbuckled his seat belt and turned to look at her.

"Do you miss it? Being a lawyer? The adrenaline rush of the courtroom and the high stakes?" she asked.

He hesitated before answering. "I'll tell you what I miss. I miss my father, who would have been proud of the man I've become over the last year. I miss the fact that I'm thirty-five years old and haven't gotten married and started a family of my own. To answer your question, no, there's absolutely nothing I miss about my old life." *Except you.*

Dear Reader,

I've been thinking a lot about heroes lately and what I
personally find attractive in a man. A rancher hero is always
sexy, a man who wears worn jeans and works the land.
But I also like a man who is equally at home in a business
suit and exudes a sense of power.

I like a man who can laugh at himself and share his laughter
with me. I hate to admit it, but I also don't mind a small
touch of bad boy in my man. He would have to possess
a passion for life and of course a passion for the woman
in his life.

Charlie Black is such a man. He's a rancher who also works
as a bodyguard. He isn't infallible; he's made some mistakes
in his life, mistakes that give him just the right touch of
humility.

As I was writing this book, I fell in love with Charlie Black.
As you read it, I hope you find yourself falling in love with
him, too.

Happy reading!

Carla Cassidy

CARLA CASSIDY

The Rancher Bodyguard

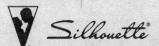

Romantic
SUSPENSE

If you purchased this book without a cover you should be aware
that this book is stolen property. It was reported as "unsold and
destroyed" to the publisher, and neither the author nor the
publisher has received any payment for this "stripped book."

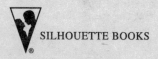

SILHOUETTE BOOKS

Recycling programs
for this product may
not exist in your area.

ISBN-13: 978-0-373-27621-9
ISBN-10:   0-373-27621-4

THE RANCHER BODYGUARD

Copyright © 2009 by Carla Bracale

All rights reserved. Except for use in any review, the reproduction
or utilization of this work in whole or in part in any form by any
electronic, mechanical or other means, now known or hereafter
invented, including xerography, photocopying and recording, or in
any information storage or retrieval system, is forbidden without
the written permission of the editorial office, Silhouette Books,
233 Broadway, New York, NY 10279 U.S.A.

This is a work of fiction. Names, characters, places and incidents are
either the product of the author's imagination or are used fictitiously, and
any resemblance to actual persons, living or dead, business establishments,
events or locales is entirely coincidental.

This edition published by arrangement with Harlequin Books S.A.

® and TM are trademarks of Harlequin Books S.A., used under license.
Trademarks indicated with ® are registered in the United States Patent
and Trademark Office, the Canadian Trade Marks Office and in other
countries.

Visit Silhouette Books at www.eHarlequin.com

Printed in U.S.A.

Books by Carla Cassidy

CARLA CASSIDY

is an award-winning author who has written more than fifty novels for Silhouette Books. In 1995, she won Best Silhouette Romance from *Romantic Times BOOKreviews* for *Anything for Danny.* In 1998, she also won a Career Achievement Award for Best Innovative Series.

Carla believes the only thing better than curling up with a good book to read is sitting down at the computer with a good story to write. She's looking forward to writing many more books and bringing hours of pleasure to readers.

Chapter 1

As he approached the barn, Charlie Black saw the sleek, scarlet convertible pulling into his driveway, and wondered when exactly, while he'd slept the night before, hell had frozen over. Because the last time he'd seen Grace Covington, that's what she'd told him would have to happen before she'd ever talk to or even look at him again.

He patted the neck of his stallion and reined in at the corral. As he dismounted and pulled off his dusty black hat, he tried to ignore the faint thrum of electricity that zinged through him as she got out of her car.

Her long blond hair sparkled in the late afternoon sun, but he was still too far away to see the expression on her lovely features.

It had been a year and a half since he'd seen her, even though for the past six months they'd resided in the same small town of Cotter Creek, Oklahoma.

The last time he'd encountered her had been in his upscale apartment in Oklahoma City. He'd been wearing a pair of sports socks and an electric blue condom. Not one of his finer moments, but it had been the culminating incident in a year of not-so-fine moments.

Too much money, too many successes and far too much booze had transformed his life into a nightmare of bad moments, the last resulting in him losing the only thing worth having.

Surely she hadn't waited all this time to come out to the family ranch—his ranch now—to finally put a bullet in what she'd described as his cold, black heart. Grace had never been the type of woman to put off till today what she could have done yesterday.

Besides, she hadn't needed a gun on that terrible Friday night when she'd arrived unannounced at his apartment. As he'd stared at her in a drunken haze, she'd given it to him with both barrels, calling him every vile name under the sun before she slammed out of his door and out of his life.

So, what was she doing here now? He slapped his horse on the rump, then motioned to a nearby ranch hand to take care of the animal. He closed the gate and approached where she hadn't moved away from the driver's side of her car.

Her hair had grown much longer since he'd last seen her. Although most of it was clasped at the back of her neck, several long wisps had escaped the confines. The beige suit she wore complemented her blond coloring and the icy blue of her eyes.

She might look cool and untouchable, like the perfect lady, but he knew what those eyes looked like flared with desire. He knew how she moaned with wild abandon when making love, and he hated the fact that just the unexpected sight of her brought back all the memories he'd worked so long and hard to forget.

"Hello, Grace," he said, as he got close enough to speak without competing with the warm April breeze. "I have to admit I'm surprised to see you. As I remember, the last time we saw each other, you indicated that hell would freeze over before you'd ever speak to me again."

Her blue eyes flashed with more than a touch of annoyance—a flash followed swiftly by a look of desperation.

"Charlie, I need you." Her low voice trembled slightly, and only then did he notice that her eyes were red-rimmed, as if she'd been weeping. In all the time they'd dated—even during the ugly scene that had ended *them*—he'd never seen her shed a single tear. "Have you heard the news?" she asked.

"What news?"

"Early this afternoon my stepfather was found stabbed to death in bed." She paused for a moment and bit her full lower lip as her eyes grew shiny with suppressed tears. "I think Hope is in trouble, Charlie. I think she's really in bad trouble."

"What?" Shock stabbed through him. Hope was

Grace's fifteen-year-old sister. He'd met her a couple of times. She'd seemed like a nice kid, not as pretty as her older sister, but a cutie nevertheless.

"Maybe you should come on inside," he said, and gestured toward the house. She stared at the attractive ranch house as if he'd just invited her into the chambers of hell. "There's nobody inside, Grace. The only woman who ever comes in is Rosa Caltano. She does the cooking and cleaning for me, and she's already left for the day."

Grace gave a curt nod and moved away from the car. She followed him to the house and up the wooden stairs to the wraparound porch.

The entry hall was just as it had been when Charlie's mother and father had been alive, with a gleaming wood floor and a dried flower wreath on the wall.

He led her to the living room. Charlie had removed much of the old furniture that he'd grown up with and replaced it with contemporary pieces in earth tones. He motioned Grace to the sofa, where she sat on the very edge as if ready to bolt at any moment. He took the chair across from her and gazed at her expectantly.

"Why do you think Hope is in trouble?"

She drew in a deep breath, obviously fighting for control. "From what I've been told, Lana, the housekeeper, found William dead in his bed. Today is her day off, but she left a sweater there last night and went back to get it. It was late enough in the day that William should have been up, so she checked on him. She immediately called Zack West, and he and some of his deputies responded. They found Hope passed out on her bed. Apparently she was the only one home at the time of the murder."

Charlie frowned, his mind reeling. Before he'd moved back here to try his hand at ranching, Charlie had been a successful, high-profile defense attorney in Oklahoma City.

It was that terrible moment in time with Grace followed by the unexpected death of his father that had made him take a good, hard look at his life and realize how unhappy he'd been for a very long time.

Still, it was as a defense attorney that he frowned at her thoughtfully. "What do you mean she was passed out? Was she asleep? Drunk?"

Those icy blue eyes of hers darkened. "Apparently she was drugged. She was taken to the hospital and is still there. They pumped her stomach and are keeping her for observation." Grace leaned forward. "Please, Charlie. Please help her. Something isn't right. First of all, Hope would never, ever take drugs, and she certainly isn't capable of something like this. She would *never* have hurt William."

Spoken like a true sister, Charlie thought. How many times had he heard family members and friends proclaim that a defendant couldn't be guilty of the crime they had been charged with, only to discover that they were wrong?

"Grace, I don't know if you've heard, but I'm a rancher now." He wasn't at all sure he wanted to get involved with any of this. It had disaster written all over it. "I've retired as a criminal defense attorney."

"I heard through the grapevine that besides being a rancher, you're working part-time with West Protective Services," she said.

"That's right," he agreed. "They approached me about a month ago and asked if I could use a little side work. It sounded intriguing, so I took them up on it, but so far I haven't done any work for them."

"Then let me hire you as Hope's bodyguard, and if you do a little criminal defense work in the process I'll pay you extra." She leaned forward, her eyes begging for his help.

Bad idea, a little voice whispered in the back of his brain. She already hated his guts, and this portended a very bad ending. He knew how much she loved her sister; he assumed that for the last couple of years she'd been more mother than sibling to the young girl. He'd be a fool to involve himself in the whole mess.

"Has Hope been questioned by anyone?" he heard himself ask. He knew he was going to get involved whether he wanted to or not, because it was Grace, because she needed him.

"I don't think so. When I left the hospital a little while ago, she was still unconscious. Dr. Dell promised me he wouldn't let anyone in to see her until I returned."

"Good." There was nothing worse than a suspect running off at the mouth with a seemingly friendly officer. Often the damage was so great there was nothing a defense attorney could do to mitigate it.

"Does that mean you'll take Hope's case?" she asked.

"Whoa," he said, and held up both his hands. "Before I agree to anything, I need to make a couple of phone calls, find out exactly what's going on and where the official investigation is headed. It's possible you don't need me, that Hope isn't in any real danger of being arrested."

"Then what happens now?"

"Why don't I plan on meeting you at the hospital in about an hour and a half? By then I'll know more of what's going on, and I'd like to be present while anybody questions Hope. If anyone asks before I get there, you tell them you're waiting for legal counsel."

She nodded and rose. She'd been lovely a year and a half ago when he'd last seen her, but she was even lovelier now.

She was five years younger than his thirty-five but had always carried herself with the confidence of an older woman. That was part of what had initially drawn him to her, that cool shell of assurance encased in a slamming hot body with the face of an angel.

"How's business at the dress shop?" he asked, trying to distract her from her troubles as he walked her back to her car. She owned a shop called Sophisticated Lady that sold designer items at discount prices. She often traveled the two-hour drive into Oklahoma City on buying trips. That was where she and Charlie had started their relationship.

They'd met in the coffee shop in the hotel where she'd been staying. Charlie had popped in to drop off some paperwork to a client and had decided to grab a cup of coffee before heading back to his office.

She'd been sitting alone next to a window. The sun had sparked on her hair. Charlie had taken one look and was smitten.

"Business is fine," she said, but it was obvious his distraction wasn't successful.

"I'm sorry about William, but Zack West is a good man, a good sheriff. He'll get to the bottom of things."

Once again she nodded and opened her car door. "Then I'll see you in the hospital in an hour and a half," she said.

"Grace?" He stopped her before she got into the seat. "Given our history, why would you come to me with this?" he asked.

Her gaze met his with a touch of frost. "Because I think Hope is in trouble and she needs a sneaky devil to make sure she isn't charged with a murder I know she didn't commit. And you, Charlie Black, are as close to the devil as I could get."

She didn't wait for his reply. She got into her car, started the engine with a roar and left him standing to eat her dust as she peeled out and back down the driveway.

Grace drove until she was out of sight of Charlie's ranch and then pulled to the side of the road. She leaned her head down on the steering wheel and fought back the tears that burned her eyes.

A nightmare. She felt as if she'd been mysteriously plunged into a nightmare and couldn't wake up to escape, didn't know how to get out.

She'd barely had time to mourn her stepfather, the man who had married her mother when she'd been sixteen and Hope had been a baby.

William Covington had not only married their mother, Elizabeth, but had also taken on her two children as if they were his own. Grace's father had died of a heart attack and William had adopted the two fatherless girls.

He'd guided Grace through the tumultuous teen years with patience and humor. He'd been their rock when their mother had simply vanished two years ago, taking with her two suitcases full of clothing and her daughters' broken hearts.

Grace raised her head from the steering wheel and pulled back on the road. She couldn't think about her mother right now. That was an old pain. She had new pains to worry about and a little sister to try to save.

No way, she thought as she headed toward the hospital. No way was Hope capable of such a heinous crime. And Hope had always been the first one to declare that she thought drugs were stupid. She couldn't be taking drugs.

But how do you know for sure? a little voice in her head whispered. She'd been so busy the last couple of years, working at the shop and flying off for buying trips. Since the disappearance of her mother and her subsequent breakup with Charlie, Grace had engaged in a frenzy of work, exhausting herself each day to keep the anger and the heartache of both her mother's and Charlie's betrayals at bay.

Sure, lately, when she'd spent time with Hope, the young girl had voiced the usual teenage complaints about William. He was too strict and old-fashioned. He gave her too little freedom and too many lectures. He hated her friends.

But those were the complaints of almost every teenager on the face of the earth, and Grace couldn't believe they had meant that Hope harbored a killing rage against William.

She turned into the hospital parking lot and slid into an empty parking space, then turned off the engine. She stared at the small structure that comprised the Cotter Creek hospital, her thoughts filled with Charlie Black.

Six months ago, everyone in town had been buzzing with the gossip that Charlie Black had finally come home. She knew his father had died from an unexpected heart attack and had left Charlie the family ranch, but she'd assumed he'd sell it and continue his self-destructive path in the fast lane. She'd been stunned to hear that he'd closed up his practice in Oklahoma City and taken over the ranch.

She'd met Charlie two months after her mother's disappearance. She hadn't told him about her mother, rather she'd used her time with him as an escape from the pain, from the utter heart break of her mother's abandonment.

With Charlie she'd been able to pretend it hadn't happened. With Charlie, for a blessed time, she'd shoved the pain deep inside her.

She'd refused to tell him because she hadn't wanted

to see pity in his eyes. She'd needed him to be her safe place away from all the madness, and for a while that's what he'd been.

As soon as she'd heard about William's murder and Hope's possible involvement, Charlie's name was the first one that had popped into her head. All the qualities she'd hated in him as a man were desirable qualities in a defense attorney.

His arrogance, his need to be right, his stubbornness and his emotional detachment made him a good defense attorney and would make him a terrific professional bodyguard, but he was definitely a poor bet for a personal relationship, as she'd discovered.

That was in the past. She didn't want anything from Charlie Black except his ability to make sure that Hope was safe.

As she got out of her car, she recognized that she was in a mild state of shock. The events of the past three hours hadn't fully caught up with her yet.

She'd been at the shop when she'd gotten the call from Deputy Ben Taylor, indicating that William was dead and Hope had been transferred to the hospital. He'd given her just enough information to both horrify and terrify her.

Her legs trembled as she made her way through the emergency room entrance. She hadn't been able to see Hope when she'd been here before, as Hope had been undergoing the stomach pumping. Surely they would let Grace see her now.

She told the nurse on duty who she was, then sat in one of the chairs in the waiting room. She was the only person there. She clasped her hands together in her lap in an attempt to stop their shaking.

Was Hope okay? Who had really killed William? He'd been a kind, gentle man. Who would want to hurt him?

She blinked back her tears and straightened her shoulders. She couldn't fall apart now. She had to be strong because she knew this was only the beginning of the nightmare.

"Grace."

She looked up to see Dr. Ralph Dell standing in the doorway. She started to stand but he motioned her back into her chair as he sat next to her. "She's stable," he said. "We pumped her stomach, but whatever she took either wasn't in pill form or had enough time to be digested. I've ordered a full toxicology screen."

"Is she conscious?" Grace asked.

"Drifting in and out. She'll be here until the effects have completely worn off." Dr. Dell eyed her soberly. "The sheriff is going to want to talk to her, and even with her condition I can keep him away only so long."

"I know. Charlie Black is supposed to meet me here in the next hour or so."

"Good. Deputy Taylor has been here since she was brought in."

Grace frowned. "Has he talked to her?"

Dr. Dell shook his head. "Up until now Hope hasn't been in any condition to talk to anyone. And I promised you I wouldn't let anyone in to see her while you were gone. I'm a man of my word."

"Thank you." Grace raised a trembling hand to her temple, where a headache had begun to pound with fierce intensity.

"How are you doing?" Dr. Dell reached out and took her hand in his. He'd been both Hope's and Grace's doctor since they'd been small girls. "You need anything, you let me know."

She realized he wasn't just holding her hand, but rather was taking her pulse at the same time. She forced a smile. "I'm okay." She withdrew her hand from his. "Really. Can I see Hope?"

He nodded his head and stood. "However, I caution you about asking her too many questions. Right now what she needs is your love and support. There will be plenty of time for answers when she's feeling more alert."

Grace heartily agreed. The last thing she wanted right now was to grill Hope about whatever might have happened at the Covington mansion that morning. All she wanted—all she *needed*—was to make sure that the sister she loved was physically all right. She'd worry about the rest later.

"I've got her in a private room," Dr. Dell said, as he led Grace down a quiet corridor.

She saw the deputy first. Ben Taylor sat in a chair in the hallway, a magazine open in his lap. He looked up as they approached, his thin face expressing no emotion as he greeted her.

"Grace." He nodded to her and shifted in his seat as if he found the whole situation awkward.

She knew Ben because his wife worked part-time

for her at the dress shop. "Hi, Ben," she replied, appalled by the shakiness of her voice.

"Bad day, huh?" He averted his gaze from hers.

"That's an understatement." There were a hundred questions she wanted to ask him, but she wasn't sure she was ready for any of the answers. Charlie would be here soon and would find out what she needed to know.

She pushed open the door of the hospital room and her heart squeezed painfully tight in her chest as she saw her sister. Hope was asleep, her petite face stark white and her blond hair a tangled mess.

Grace wanted to bundle her up in the sheet, pick her up and run out the door. Nobody could ever make her believe that Hope had anything to do with William's murder.

Pulling up a chair next to Hope's bed, Grace fought against a tremendous amount of guilt. In the past couple of months had she been too absent from Hope's life? Had there been things she wasn't aware of, things that had led to this terrible crime?

Stop it, she commanded herself. She was thinking as if Hope was guilty, and she wasn't. She wasn't! As soon as Charlie arrived, everything would be okay.

A knot of simmering anger twisted in her stomach. She shouldn't be alone here, waiting for Hope to wake up. Their mother should be with her, but she'd run from her responsibility and her family and disappeared like a puff of smoke on a windy day. Hope had been far too young to lose her mother. *Damn you, Mom,* Grace thought.

Hope stirred and her eyes opened. She frowned and looked at Grace in obvious confusion. "Sis?" Her voice was a painful croak.

Grace leaned forward and grabbed Hope's hand. "I'm here, honey. It's all right. You're going to be all right now."

Hope looked around wildly, as if unsure where she was. Her gaze locked with Grace's once again, and in the depths of Hope's eyes Grace saw a whisper of terror. "What happened?"

"You got your stomach pumped. Did you take something, Hope? Some kind of drug?"

Hope's eyes flashed with annoyance and she rose to a half-sitting position. "I don't do drugs. Drugs are for losers." She fell back against the bed and closed her eyes, as if the brief conversation had completely exhausted her.

Grace remained seated next to her, clasping her hand even after she realized Hope had fallen back asleep. If Hope hadn't taken any drugs, then why had the authorities found her unconscious on her bed when they'd arrived?

Had she been hit over the head? Knocked unconscious by whoever had committed the murder? Surely if she'd had a head injury Dr. Dell would have found it.

Hope slept the sleep of the drugged, not awakening even when a nurse came in to take her vital signs. The nurse didn't speak to Grace. She simply did her job with stern lips pressed tightly together.

Minutes ticked by with nauseating slowness.

Grace checked her watch over and over again, wondering when Charlie would arrive. Hopefully he'd
have some answers that would unravel the knot of
dread tied tight in her stomach.

She leaned her head back against the chair and
thought of Charlie. The moment she'd seen him
again, an electric charge had sizzled through her. It
had surprised her.

He was as handsome now as he'd been when
they'd dated, his dark hair rich and full and his
features aristocratically elegant, holding just a hint
of danger. She knew those slate-gray eyes of his
could narrow with cold intent or stoke a fire so hot
a woman felt as if she might combust.

She'd been more than half in love with him when
they'd broken up. She'd thought he felt the same
way about her, but the redhead in his bed that night
had told her different.

On that night she'd hated him more than she'd
loved him, and in the past eighteen months her
feelings hadn't changed. She rubbed her fingers
across her forehead, thoughts of Charlie Black only
increasing her headache.

Maybe he'd come in and tell her that Hope wasn't
in any trouble, didn't need the expertise of a criminal
defense lawyer or a bodyguard. Then she'd go back
to the mess that had suddenly become her life and
never see Charlie again.

She glanced at her watch and frowned. He was
late. He was always late. That was something else

she'd always found irritating about him—his inability to be on time for anything.

She didn't know why she was thinking about him anyway, except that it was far easier to think about Charlie than what had happened.

Somebody murdered William. Somebody murdered William. The words thundered through her brain in perfect rhythm with her pounding headache.

Who would want him dead? He'd been a wealthy man, a generous benefactor to numerous charities. He'd been well liked in the community and loved and respected by the two stepdaughters he'd claimed as his own.

Although he was the CEO of several industrial companies, he'd stopped working full-time a year ago and went in only occasionally for meetings.

He was kind and gentle, and his heart had been broken when Hope and Grace's mother had left him, left *them.* Tears burned her eyes again and she struggled to hold them back as she realized she'd never again see his gentle smile, never again feel the touch of his hand on her shoulder.

It was just after seven when the hospital door creaked open and Charlie motioned her out of the room. She got up from the chair and joined him in the hallway, where he took her by the arm and led her away from Ben Taylor.

"We've got a problem," he said when they were far enough down the hallway that Ben couldn't hear their conversation. His gray eyes were like granite slabs, revealing nothing of his thoughts.

"What?" she asked.

"I have every reason to believe that as soon as Hope is well enough to be released by the doctor, she's going to be arrested for the murder of your stepfather."

Grace gasped. "But why? How could anyone think she's responsible?"

He shifted his gaze and stared at some point just over her head. "Hope wasn't just found passed out on her bed. Her room had been trashed as if she'd been in a fit of rage."

"But that doesn't make her a murderer," Grace exclaimed. Although it *was* definitely out of character for Hope to do something like that. Hope had always been a neatnik who loved her room neat and tidy.

Charlie sighed and focused his gaze back on her. The darkness she saw there terrified her. "The real problem is that Hope was found covered in William's blood—and she had a knife in her hand. It was the murder weapon."

Chapter 2

Charlie watched as the color left Grace's cheeks and she swayed on her feet. His first impulse was to reach out to her, but before he could follow through, she stiffened and took a step back from him.

She'd never been a needy woman—that was one of the things he'd always admired about her and ultimately one of the things he'd come to hate. That she wasn't needy—that she had never really needed him.

"So, what do we do now?" Her strong voice gave away nothing of the emotional turmoil she must be feeling.

"Zack West wants to question her tonight. I just saw him in the lobby and he's chomping at the bit to get to her. Give me a dollar."

"Excuse me?" She looked at him blankly.

"Give me a dollar as a retainer. That will make it official that at least for now, I'm Hope's legal counsel. She's a minor. She can't be questioned without me, and we can argue that as her legal guardian you have the right to be present, too."

She opened her purse and withdrew a crisp dollar bill. He took it from her and shoved it into his back pocket. "I'll go find Zack and we'll get this over with."

As he walked away, her scent lingered in his head. She'd always smelled like jasmine and the faintest hint of vanilla, and today was no different.

It was a scent that had stayed with him for months after she'd left him, a fragrance that had once smelled like desire and had wound up smelling like regret.

This was a fool's job, and he was all kinds of fool for getting involved. From what little he'd already learned, it didn't look good for the young girl.

If he got involved and ended up defending Hope, then failed, Grace would have yet another reason to hate his guts. Even if he defended Hope successfully, that wasn't a ticket to the land of forgiveness where Grace was concerned.

Still, Charlie knew that in all probability Hope was going to need a damn good lawyer on her side, and he was just arrogant enough to believe that he was the best in the four-state area.

Besides, he owed it to Grace. Although at the time of their breakup they'd been not only on different pages but in completely different books, he'd never forgotten the rich, raw pain on her face when she'd been confronted by the knowledge that he hadn't been monogamous.

Maybe fate had given him this opportunity to right the wrong, to heal some wounds and assuage the guilt he'd felt ever since.

He found Zack in the waiting room. The handsome sheriff was pacing the floor and frowning. He stopped in his tracks as Charlie approached him. "If you want to question Hope, then Grace and I intend to be present," Charlie said.

Zack raised a dark eyebrow. "Are you here as Hope's lawyer?"

"Maybe." Charlie replied.

Zack sighed. "You going to make this difficult for me?"

"Probably," Charlie replied dryly. "You can't really believe that Hope killed William."

"Right now, I'm just in the information-gathering mode. After I have all the information I need, *then* I can decide if I have a viable suspect or not."

Zack had only been sheriff for less than a year, but Charlie knew he was a truth seeker and not a town pleaser. He would look for justice, not make a fast arrest in order to waylay the fears of the people in Cotter Creek. But if all the evidence pointed to Hope, Zack would have no choice but to arrest her.

"I heard you were working for Dalton," Zack said.

Dalton was Zack's brother and ran the family business, West Protective Services, an agency that provided bodyguard services around the country.

"I told him I'd be interested in helping out

whenever he needed me," Charlie replied. "But I need to get this situation under control before I do anything else."

"Then let's do it," Zack said. He headed down the hallway toward Hope's room and Charlie followed close behind.

Dr. Dell met them at her door, his arms crossed over his chest like a mythical guardian of a magical jewel. "I know you have a job to do here, Sheriff, but so do I. She's still very weak, so I want this interview to be short and sweet."

Zack nodded, and the doctor stepped away. Grace's eyes narrowed slightly as Zack and Charlie entered the room. She sat next to the bed, where Hope was awake.

The kid looked sick and terrified as her gaze swept from Charlie to Zack. "Hope, you remember Zack West, the sheriff," Grace said. "And Charlie is here as your lawyer."

Hope's eyes widened, and Charlie had a feeling she hadn't realized just what kind of trouble she was in until this moment. Tears filled her eyes and she reached for her sister's hand.

"I want to ask you some questions," Zack said. He pulled a small tape recorder from his pocket and set it on the nightstand next to the bed. "You mind if I turn this on?"

Hope looked wildly at Charlie, who nodded his assent. Charlie stood next to Grace, trying to ignore the way her evocative scent made him remember the pleasure of making love with her and how crazy he'd been about her.

He couldn't think about that now—he knew he shouldn't think about that ever again. He couldn't go back and change the past and that terrible mistake he'd made. All he could do was step up right now and hopefully redeem himself just a little bit.

"I told her about William," Grace said to Zack, her chin lifted in a gesture of defiance. "She knows he was murdered but insists she had nothing to do with it."

A knot of tension formed in Zack's jaw. "I need to hear from her what happened today," he said, and focused his gaze on Hope. "What's the first thing you remember from this morning?"

Hope raised a trembling hand to her head and rubbed her temples. "I woke up around nine and went downstairs to get some breakfast. Nobody was around. It was Lana's day off, and I figured William was still in bed. Lately he'd been sleeping in longer than usual."

She stopped talking as tears once again filled her blue eyes. "I can't believe he's gone. I just don't understand any of this. Why would somebody do this to him? What happened to me?"

"So, you made yourself breakfast, then what did you do?" Zack asked, seemingly unmoved by her tears.

Grace's lips were a thin slash, and her pretty features were taut with tension. Several more strands of her shiny blond hair had escaped her barrette and framed her face.

Charlie was surprised to realize he wanted to do something, anything to erase that apprehensive look on her face, to alleviate the tortured shadows in her eyes.

"After I ate breakfast, I was still tired, so I went

back to bed," Hope replied. "And I woke up here." Her features crumbled. "I don't know what happened to William. I don't know what happened to me." She began to cry in earnest, deep, wrenching sobs.

Grace got up from her chair and put her arms around Hope's slender shoulders and glared at Zack as if he were personally responsible for all the unhappiness on the entire planet.

"Isn't this enough?" she asked, those blue eyes of hers filled with anger. "Can't you see what this is doing to her?"

Unfortunately, Charlie knew that Zack was just getting started. "Grace, let's just get this over with," he said. "Zack has to question her sooner or later. We might as well get it finished now. We'll give her a minute to pull herself together."

Zack waited until Hope calmed down a bit before asking about any tensions between her and William and probing her about any fights her stepfather might have had with anyone else.

Charlie protested only a couple of times when he thought the questions Zack asked might incriminate Hope if she answered.

Despite Charlie's efforts to protect Hope, what little information Zack got from the girl offered no alternative suspect and merely added to the mystery of what exactly happened in the Covington mansion that morning.

After an hour and a half of questioning, it was Grace who finally called a halt to the interrogation. "That's enough for tonight, Zack," she said firmly, as she rose from her chair. "Hope is exhausted. She isn't going anywhere. If you have more questions for her, you can ask them another time."

Zack nodded and reached over and turned off the tape recorder, then slipped the small device into his pocket. "I'll be in touch. I guess I don't have to tell you and Hope not to leave town."

"Innocent people don't leave town," she replied vehemently.

Zack left the room and Grace leaned over her sister. "We're going to go now, honey. We need to take care of some things. Nobody will bother you for the rest of the night. Just get some sleep and try not to worry. Charlie is going to fix all this, so there's nothing to worry about."

Charlie nearly groaned out loud. Sure, that was easy for her to say. But he was a defense attorney turned rancher, not a miracle worker.

They left the room together, and once out in the hallway Grace slumped against the polished wall. For the first time since arriving at his ranch, she looked lost and achingly fragile.

His need to touch her—to somehow chase away that vulnerable look in her eyes—was incredibly strong. "Do you need a hug?" The ridiculous words were out of his mouth before he'd realized he was going to say them.

She released a bitter laugh and shoved off the wall. "I'd rather hug a rattlesnake," she said thinly.

If he had any question about the depth of her dislike for him, her curt reply certainly answered it.

"It doesn't look good, does it?" she asked.

"It doesn't look great," he replied.

"So what happens now?" she inquired, as they continued down the hallway to the hospital's front doors.

"Nothing for now. Questioning Hope is only the beginning. We really won't know how much trouble she's in until Zack's completed his investigation into the murder."

They stepped out into the unusually warm spring night air, and again he caught a whiff of her sweet floral scent. He wanted to ask her if she was dating anyone, if she'd found love with somebody else in the eighteen months since they'd been together.

He reminded himself he had no right to know anything about her personal life, that he'd given up any such right the night he'd gotten drunk and fallen into bed with a woman whose name he couldn't even remember.

"I don't want to wait for Zack," she said. "I want us to investigate this murder just as vigorously as he will."

Charlie looked at her in surprise. "That's a crazy idea!" he exclaimed.

"Why is it crazy? You told me once that you worked as an investigator before you became a lawyer."

"That was a long time ago," he reminded her.

She crossed her arms, a mutinous expression on her face. "Fine, then I'll investigate it on my own." She turned on her heels and walked off.

Charlie sighed in frustration. "Grace, wait," he

called after her. "I can't let you muck around in this alone. You could potentially do more damage than good for Hope."

"Then help me," she said, her voice low with desperation. "I'm all that Hope has. The only way to make sure she isn't railroaded for a crime she didn't commit is for me to find the guilty person, and that's exactly what I intend to do—with or without your help." She paused, her eyes glittering darkly. "So, are you going to help me or not?"

He shoved his hands in his jeans pocket and shook his head. "I'd forgotten just how stubborn you could be."

"I don't think you want to start pointing out character flaws in other people," she said pointedly.

To Charlie's surprise, he felt the warmth of a flush heat his cheeks. "Touché," he said. "All right, we'll do a little digging of our own. The first thing you should do is make a list of William's friends and business associates. We need to pick his life apart if we hope to find some answers."

"I can have a list for you by tomorrow. Why don't you meet me at my shop around noon, and we can decide exactly where to go from there."

"You're going into work?" he asked in surprise.

"I'd rather meet you at the shop than at my place," she replied.

"All right, then, tomorrow at noon," he agreed reluctantly. Charlie had worked extremely hard over the last six months to gain control and now felt his life was suddenly whirling back out of control.

She nodded. "Charlie, you should know that just because I came to you for help—just because I need you right now—doesn't mean I like you. When this is all over, I don't want to see you again." She turned and left without waiting for a response.

Jeez, he seemed to be watching her walking away from him a lot, especially after throwing a bomb at him. Still, he couldn't help but notice the sexy sway of those hips beneath the suit skirt and the length of her shapely legs. A surge of familiar regret welled up inside him.

He was a man who made few excuses or apologies for the choices he made, but the mistake of throwing Grace away would haunt him until the day he died.

The morning sun was shining brightly as Grace parked in front of her dress shop on Main Street. She turned off the engine but remained seated in the car, her thoughts still on the visit she'd just had with Hope.

Hope had been no less confused about the events of the day before and didn't seem to understand that at the moment she was the best suspect they had.

Fortunately, Dr. Dell wanted to keep her under observation for another twenty-four hours, and that was fine with Grace. The tox screen had come back showing a cocktail of drugs in Hope's system but Hope was still vehemently denying taking anything. At the hospital, Hope was safe and getting the best care.

Grace wearily rubbed a hand across her forehead. The day was just beginning, and she was already exhausted. Her sleep had been a continuous reel of nightmares.

She'd been haunted by visions of Hope stabbing William and then taking the drugs that knocked her unconscious. And if that hadn't been bad enough, images of Charlie also filled her dreams.

Charlie. She got out of the car and slammed the door harder than necessary, as if doing so could cast out all thoughts of the man.

She focused her attention on the shop before her. Sophisticated Lady had been a dream of hers from the time she was small. She'd always loved fashion and design, and five years ago for her twenty-fifth birthday, William had loaned her the money to open the shop.

Grace had worked her tail off to stock the store with fine clothing at discount prices, and within two years she'd managed to pay back the loan and expand into accessories and shoes.

Now all she could think about was whether she'd sacrificed her sister's well-being for making her shop a success. She'd spent long hours here at the store, and when she wasn't here she was away on buying trips or at Charlie's place for the weekend.

As much as she hated to admit it, she didn't know what had been going on in Hope's life lately, but she intended to find out.

She entered the shop, turned on the lights and went directly to the back office, where she made a pot of coffee. With a cup of fresh brew in hand, she returned to the sales floor and sat on the stool behind the counter that held the register.

Much of her time the night before had been spent thinking about William, grieving for him while at the same time trying to figure out who might want him dead. The list of potential suspects she had to give to Charlie was frighteningly short.

The morning was unusually quiet. No customers had entered when Dana Taylor came through the door at eleven-thirty. "Hey, Grace," she said, her tone unusually somber. "How are you holding up?"

"As well as can be expected," Grace replied. "Right now I'm having trouble wrapping my mind around it all."

"I'm so sorry," Dana replied sympathetically.

"I was wondering if maybe you'd be available to take some extra hours for a while. I'm going to be busy with other things."

"Not a problem," Dana replied, as she stowed her purse under the counter. "When Ben got home from the hospital last night, he told me not to expect to see a lot of him for the next week or two." She didn't quite meet Grace's eyes.

"There's a new shipment of handbags in the back. If you have time this afternoon, could you unpack them and get them on display?" Grace asked, desperate to get over the awkwardness of the moment.

"Sure," Dana agreed. "Any business this morning?"

"Nothing. It's been quiet." Grace turned toward the door as it opened to admit Charlie.

An intense burst of electricity shot through her at the sight of him, and instantly every defense she possessed went up.

"Morning, ladies," he said as he ambled toward the counter. Clad in a pair of snug jeans and a short-sleeved white shirt, he looked half rancher, half businessman and all handsome male.

His square jaw indicated a hint of stubbornness and his eyes were fringed with long, dark lashes. His nose was straight, his lips full enough to give women fantasies of kissing them. In short, Charlie was one hot hunk.

His energy filled the air, and despite her wishes to the contrary, Grace felt a crazy surge of warmth as she gazed at him.

"Good morning, Charlie," Dana replied. "How are things out at the ranch?"

"Not bad. The cattle are getting fat, and I've got a garden full of tomato and pepper plants that are going to yield blue-ribbon-quality product."

Pride rang in his voice, a pride that surprised Grace. Two years ago, the only things that put that kind of emotion in his voice were his fancy surround-sound system, his state-of-the-art television and the new Italian shoes that cost what most people earned in a month.

He turned his gaze to Grace. "We need to talk," he said. His smile was gone, and the enigmatic look in his gray eyes created a knot in Grace's stomach.

"Okay. Come on back to my office," she said.

He followed her to the back room, where she turned and looked at him. "Something else has happened?"

"No, I just have some new information."

"What kind of information?" She leaned against the

desk, needing the support because she knew with certainty whatever he was about to tell her wasn't good.

"Did you know that Hope has a boyfriend?" he asked.

She frowned. "Hope is only fifteen. Their relationship can't be anything serious."

One of his dark eyebrows quirked upward. "When you're fifteen, everything is serious. His name is Justin Walker. Do you know him?"

Grace shook her head, and a new shaft of guilt pierced through her. She should have known her sister's boyfriend. What other things didn't she know? "So, who is he?"

"He's a seventeen-year-old high school dropout with a bad reputation," Charlie replied. "And there's more. Apparently Justin was a bone of contention between William and Hope. William thought he was too old and was bad news and had forbidden Hope from seeing him."

Grace sat on the edge of her desk. "How did you find out all of this?"

"I had a brief conversation with Zack this morning. I wanted to be up-to-date on where the investigation was going before meeting you today. And there's more."

She eyed him narrowly. "I'm really beginning to hate those words."

"Then you're really going to hate this," he said. "On the night before the murder, Hope and William went out to dinner at the café. An employee told Zack that while there, they had a public argument ending with Hope screaming that she wished he were dead."

Grace's heart plummeted to her feet, and she wished she didn't hate Charlie, because at the moment she wanted nothing more than his big strong arms around her.

Chapter 3

Justin Walker lived with a buddy in the Majestic Apartments complex on the outskirts of town. The illustrious name of the apartments had to have been somebody's idea of a very bad joke.

The small complex had faded from yellow to a weathered gray from the Oklahoma sun and sported several broken windows. The vehicles in the parking lot ran the gamut from souped-up hot rods to a rusty pickup truck missing two tires.

"You sure you want to do this?" Charlie asked dubiously, as he parked in front of the building and cut his engine.

Grace stared at the building in obvious dismay. "Not really, but it has to be done. I want to know exactly what his relationship with Hope was…is. I want to hear it from him, and then I want to hear it from my sister." She turned to look at Charlie. "Does he work?"

"He's a mechanic down at the garage, but he called in sick this morning."

"You managed to learn a lot between last night and now," she observed.

He shrugged and pulled his keys from the ignition. "It just took a phone call to find out if he was at the garage today. Somehow I knew you'd want to talk to him." He directed his gaze back at the building. "But, just because he isn't at work doesn't mean he's here."

"There's only one way to find out." She opened her car door and stepped out.

Charlie joined her on the cracked sidewalk and tried not to notice how pretty she looked in the yellow skirt that showcased her shapely legs and the yellow-flowered blouse that hugged her slender curves.

This whole thing would have been so much easier if during the time they'd been apart she sprouted some facial hair or maybe grown a wart on the end of her nose.

"Which unit is it?" she asked.

"Unit four." He pointed to the corner apartment, one that sported a broken window. Grace grimaced but marched with determined strides toward the door, on which she knocked in a rapid staccato fashion.

Charlie stepped in between her and the front door, protective instincts coming into play. He had no idea if Justin was just a loser boyfriend or an active participant in William's murder.

The door opened and a tall young man gazed at them with a wealth of belligerence. He looked like he wasn't having a good day. "Are you more cops?" he asked, his dark eyes wary and guarded.

Grace moved closer to the door. "No. I'm Grace Covington, Hope's sister, and this is her lawyer, Charlie Black. Are you Justin?"

He hesitated a moment, as if considering whether or not to tell the truth, then gave a curt nod of his head, his dark hair flopping carelessly onto his forehead. "Yeah, I'm Justin. What do you want?"

"Sheriff West has already talked to you?" Charlie asked.

Justin's eyes darkened. "He was here half the night asking me questions."

"May we come in?" Grace asked.

Justin's eyes swept the length of her and he scowled. "You don't want to come in here. The place is a dump." He stepped outside and closed the door behind him.

"You were dating my sister?" Grace asked.

Justin barked a dry laugh. "I wouldn't exactly call it dating. She's not allowed to date until she turns sixteen. We hung out, that's all. When she'd show up down at the garage after school, I'd take a break and we'd just talk. It was no big deal."

There was hostility in his voice, as if he expected them to take issue with him. "Were you sleeping with her?" Grace asked. Charlie wasn't sure who was more surprised by the question, himself or Justin.

Justin gave her a mocking smile. "Don't worry, big sister. As far as I know your baby sister is still as pure as the driven snow."

"Where were you yesterday morning?" Charlie asked. "Your boss told me you weren't at work." He felt Grace stiffen next to him.

"Funny, the sheriff asked me the same thing." Justin clutched his stomach. "I've been fighting off this flu bug. Yesterday I was here in bed, and if you don't believe me, my roommate will vouch for me. I didn't leave here all day."

"And your roommate's name?" Charlie asked.

Justin stepped back toward his apartment door. "Sam Young, and now I'm done answering your questions." He stepped back inside and shut the door firmly in their faces.

"Do you believe him?" Grace asked when they were back in Charlie's car and headed for the hospital.

He cast her a wry glance. "In the words of a famous television personality, I wouldn't believe him if his tongue came notarized."

Her burst of laughter was short-lived, but the sound of it momentarily warmed his heart. Charlie always loved to hear her laugh, and there had been a time when he'd been good at making her do so.

"After we speak with Hope, I need to find out if I can go to the house and get some of her things," Grace said. "Dr. Dell thought he would release her at some point this evening or first thing in the morning, and we'll need to get some of her clothes and things to take to my place."

"When we get to the hospital, I'll call Zack and see what can be arranged."

"I'd like to talk to Hope alone. I don't think she'll be open about her relationship with Justin if you're there, too."

"Okay," he replied. He glanced at her and caught her rubbing her temple. "Headache?"

She nodded and dropped her hand back into her lap. "I think it's a guilt thing."

"Guilt? What do you have to feel guilty about?" he asked in surprise.

A tiny frown danced across her forehead, doing nothing to detract from her attractiveness. "I should have been paying more attention to what was going on in her life. I should have been putting in less hours at the store and spending more time with her."

"Regrets are funny things, Grace. They rip your heart out, but they don't really change anything," he replied. He was an old hand at entertaining regrets.

"You're right." She reached up, massaged her temple once again and then shot him a pointed look. "You're absolutely right. The past is over and nothing can change the damage done. What's important is to learn from the mistakes made in the past and never forget the lesson."

Charlie frowned, knowing her words were barbs flung at him and had nothing to do with the situation at hand. They spoke no more until they arrived at the hospital.

As she disappeared into Hope's hospital room, he called Zack West to find out what was going on at the Covington mansion. Zack informed him that the evidence gathering was finished and said Grace was free to get whatever she needed for Hope.

When Charlie asked him for an update, he merely replied that it was an ongoing investigation and there was nothing new to report.

As he waited for Grace, he sat in one of the plastic chairs in the waiting room. Charlie had a theory that murder happened for one of three reasons. He called it his "three *R*" theory. Rage, revenge and reward were the motives that drove most murderers.

At the moment, the officials were leaning toward rage—a young girl's rage at being stymied in a love relationship by an overbearing father figure.

The news was certainly filled with stories of young people going on killing rampages against authority figures. Had Hope snapped that morning and stabbed William while he slept and then, filled with remorse, taken drugs in a suicide attempt?

Hopefully they would be successful in coming up with an alternative theory that would explain both William's death and Hope's drugged state.

He looked up as Grace entered the room. She sat next to him as if too exhausted to stand. "What did she have to say about Justin?" he asked.

"She told me she's crazy in love with him, and she thinks they belong together forever, but she hasn't gotten physical with him yet."

"That's different from Justin's story. He made it

sound like she was no big deal to him," Charlie observed.

"Maybe he doesn't feel the same way she does. Maybe he was afraid to tell us how he really feels about Hope," she replied.

"Maybe," Charlie agreed.

Grace reached up and tucked a strand of her shiny hair behind her ear. "She's not being released today. She's running a fever and Dr. Dell wants to get to the bottom of it."

"You still want to go by the house?" She sat so close to him he could feel the heat from her body. He used to tease her about how she was better than a hot water bottle at keeping him warm on cold wintry nights. He wished he could tell her how he'd been cold ever since he'd lost her.

She nodded. "Whether she's here or at my place, I'm sure she'd be more comfortable with some of her own things. Besides, I'd like to talk to Lana, William's housekeeper. She'd know better than anyone what was going on between William and Hope, and if anyone else was having a problem with William."

Grace jumped up from the chair, newfound energy vibrating from her. "We need to find something, Charlie, something that will point the finger of guilt away from Hope. I can't lose her. She's all I have left."

She looked half frantic, and again a soft vulnerability sagged her shoulders and haunted her eyes. This time Charlie didn't fight his impulse—his need to touch her. He reached out for her hand and took it in his. Hers was icy, as if the heat of her body was unable to warm her small, trembling hand.

"We'll figure it out," he said. "I promise you that we'll get to the bottom of this. I won't let Hope be convicted of a crime she didn't commit."

What he didn't say was that if Hope was guilty, not even the great Charlie Black would be able to save her.

The Covington estate was located on the northern edge of town, a huge two-story structure with mani-cured grounds, several outbuildings and a small cottage in the back where Lana Racine and her husband, Leroy, lived.

As Charlie pulled into the circular drive and parked in front, Grace stared at the big house and felt the burgeoning grief welling up inside her.

The sight of the bright yellow crime-scene tape across the front door nearly made her lose control, but she didn't. She couldn't.

She'd spent her life being the strong one—the child her mother could depend on, the teenager who often took responsibility for her baby sister, and the woman who'd held it together when her mother deserted them.

Charlie didn't know about her mother. When they'd been dating, she told him only that her mother had moved away, not that she'd just packed her bags and disappeared from their lives.

Without an explanation.

Without a word since.

Was she sunning on a beach in Florida? Eating

crab cakes and lobster in Maine? Or was she out of the country? She'd always talked about wanting to go to France.

Grace welcomed the raw anger that took the place of her grief—it sustained her, kept her strong.

She glanced back at Charlie, wondering if she should tell him about what had been going on in her life when she'd met him. She dismissed the idea. She couldn't stand the idea of seeing pity in his eyes, and after all this time, what difference did it make?

"Are you sure you're ready to go in there?" Charlie asked.

She focused back on the house and nodded. "I'll just get some of Hope's things, then we can go talk with Lana and Leroy."

She almost wished Charlie weren't here with her. He'd stirred old feelings in her, made her remember how much she'd once cared about him. She'd thought her hatred of him would protect her from those old feelings—that it would vaccinate her against the "wanting Charlie" emotion. She'd been wrong.

All day she'd been plagued by memories of the taste of his lips on hers, the feel of his hands stroking the length of her. Their physical relationship had been nothing short of magic. He'd been an amazing lover, at times playful and at other times intense and demanding.

But it wasn't just those kinds of memories that bothered her. Remembering how often they had laughed together and how much they'd enjoyed each other's company had proved equally troubling.

Amnesia would have been welcome. She would have loved to permanently forget the six months with Charlie, but spending time with him now unlocked the mental box in which she'd placed those memories the night she'd walked away from him.

Focus on the reason he's in your life, she told herself. Hope. She had to stay focused on Hope and finding something, anything, that would reveal the young girl's innocence.

She got out of the car, grateful to escape the small confines that smelled of him—a wonderful blend of clean male and expensive, slightly spicy cologne. It was the same scent he'd worn when they'd been dating, and it only helped stir memories she would prefer to forget.

Charlie pulled away the crime-scene tape, and Grace used her key to open the front door. They walked into the massive entry with its marble floor and an ornate gilded mirror hanging on the wall.

"Wow," Charlie said, obviously impressed. "I'd heard this place was a showcase, but I had no idea."

"William was an extremely successful man," she replied. "He liked to surround himself with beautiful things."

"I know you said your mother married him when you were sixteen. What happened to your father?"

"He died of a heart attack when mom was pregnant with Hope. We were left with no insurance and no money in the bank." Grace paused a moment, thinking about those days just after her father's death. There'd been a wealth of grief and fear about what would happen to them now the breadwinner was gone.

She walked from the entry to the sweeping stair-case that led to the second floor. Placing a hand on the polished wood banister, she continued: "William was like a knight in shining armor. He and Mom met at the grocery store, and he swooped into our lives like a savior. He was crazy, not just about Mom, but also about me and Hope."

"He didn't have children of his own?" Charlie asked.

"No. He'd been married years before, but it ended in divorce and there had been no children. We were all the family he had."

"Who is his beneficiary?"

Grace looked at him in surprise. "I have no idea. I hadn't even thought about it."

"Maybe your mother?" he asked.

"Maybe," Grace agreed, although she wasn't so sure. Grace's mother had ripped the very heart out of William when she'd disappeared. William had been a good man, generous to a fault, but he hadn't been a foolish man, especially when it came to money.

"Let's get Hope's things and get out of here," she said, her heart heavy as she climbed the stairs.

Charlie followed just behind her as she topped the stairs and walked down the long hallway toward Hope's room. The door was closed and she hesi-tated, unsure she was ready for whatever was inside.

Hope had been found covered in blood, clutching the knife in her hands, her room trashed. Grace grabbed the doorknob and still couldn't force herself to open the door.

Charlie placed a hand on her shoulder. "We don't have to do this. We can buy Hope whatever she needs for the time being."

How could a man who had been incredibly insensitive eighteen months ago, a man who had been so thick he hadn't recognized the depths of her feelings for him, be so in tune to what she was feeling now?

She didn't have the answer but was grateful that he seemed to understand the turmoil inside her as she contemplated going into Hope's room. Deep within, she knew she was grateful that he was here with her.

"It's all right. I can do this," she said, as much to herself as to him.

She straightened her shoulders and opened the door. A gasp escaped her as she saw the utter mess inside. She took several steps into the room and stared around in horror.

Ripped clothes were everywhere. The French provincial bookshelf had been turned over, spilling its contents onto the floor. A hole was punched in the Sheetrock wall, as if it had been angrily kicked.

The bed had been stripped. She imagined that the investigators had taken away the bedclothes. "Definitely looks like somebody had a temper fit in here," Charlie said from behind her.

Grace's mind whirled with sick suppositions. Was it possible that a rage had been festering in Hope for some time? Their mother's defection had been difficult on Grace, but it had been devastating for Hope. Grace had been twenty-eight years old when their mother had left, but Hope had been a thirteen-year-old who desperately needed her mom.

"I'll just grab some clothes," Grace said. She'd taken only two steps toward the closet when her foot crunched on something.

She looked down and saw the arm of a porcelain doll. She knew that arm. She knew that doll. It had been Hope's prized possession, given to her on the birthday before their mother had disappeared.

Crouching down, she found the rest of the doll among the mess of clothes and books and miscellaneous items that had fallen from the bookcase.

The porcelain arms and legs had been pulled from the cloth body. The head was smashed beyond repair, and the body had been slashed open.

Rage. There was no doubt that rage had destroyed the doll. The rage of a daughter whose mother had left her with a man who hadn't been able to understand her needs, her wants?

Hope's rage?

The breakdown that began in Grace started with a trembling that seemed to possess her entire body. Her vision blurred with the hot press of tears, and for the first time she wondered if her sister had committed the crime, if it was possible that Hope was guilty.

Chapter 4

Charlie saw it coming: the crack in her strength, the loss of her control. Until this moment Grace had shown an incredible amount of poise in dealing with the mess that had become her life.

Now she looked up at him with tear-filled eyes and lips that trembled uncontrollably, and he knew she'd reached the end of that strength.

"Grace." He said her name softly.

"She couldn't have done this, Charlie? Surely she didn't do this?" They weren't statements of fact but questions of uncertainty, and he knew the agony the doubts must be causing her.

Again the crazy, overwhelming need to hold her, to be her soft place to fall, swept over him. He touched her shoulder, then placed his hand beneath her arm to help her to her feet.

The tears in her eyes streamed down her cheeks, and when Charlie wrapped his arms around her, she didn't fight the embrace—she fell into it.

Her body fit perfectly against his, molding to him with sweet familiarity. A rush of emotions filled him—compassion because of the ordeal she was going through, fear for what she might have to face, and finally a desire for her that he couldn't deny.

The vanilla scent of her hair coupled with that familiar jasmine fragrance filled his head, making him half dizzy.

The embrace was over soon after it began. Grace jumped back as if stung by the physical contact. "I'm okay," she exclaimed as a stain of color spread across her cheeks.

"I never thought otherwise," he replied dryly. He'd be a fool to think that it had been *his* arms she'd needed around her, *his* comfort she'd sought. She'd just needed a little steadying, and if it hadn't been him, it would have been anyone.

She didn't need steadying anymore. Her shoulders were once again rigid as she went around the room, gathering clothes in her arms. After he took the clothes from her, she went into the adjoining bathroom and returned a moment later with a small overnight bag he assumed held toiletries.

"That should do it," she said. Any hint of tears was gone from her eyes, and they once again shone with the steely strength they'd always possessed.

They left the bedroom and went back down the stairs. She relocked the front door, then they stowed Hope's things in the car and headed back to the caretaker cottage where Lana and Leroy Racine lived.

If Charlie was going to mount a credible defense for Hope, he knew that to create reasonable doubt he had to identify another potential suspect with a motive for murder.

He'd never met the Racines, and as he and Grace walked across the lush grass to the cottage in the distance, he asked her some questions about the couple.

"How long have Lana and Leroy worked for William?"

"Lana was William's housekeeper when my mother married him. She married Leroy about ten years ago and soon after had their son, Lincoln."

"Leroy works the grounds?" he asked.

She nodded. "William hired him when he and Lana got married. As you can see, he does a great job."

"Theirs is a happy marriage?"

She shrugged. "I assume so. I'm not exactly privy to their personal life, but they seem very happy. They're both crazy about Lincoln."

They fell silent as they reached the house. It was an attractive place, painted pristine white with black shutters. The porch held two rocking chairs and several pots of brilliant flowers.

Grace knocked on the door, and an attractive redhaired woman who looked to be in her forties answered. She took one look at Grace and broke into torrential sobs.

Grace's eyes misted once again, and she quickly embraced the woman in a hug. "I can't believe it," Lana cried. "I just can't believe he's gone."

"I know. I feel the same way," Grace replied.

Lana stepped away from her and dabbed at her eyes with a tissue from her pocket. "Come in, please." She ushered them into a small but neat and tidy living room, where Grace introduced Charlie.

"Would you like something? Maybe something to drink?" Lana asked as she motioned for them to sit in the two chairs across from the sofa.

"No thanks. We're fine. I wanted to ask you some questions," Grace said. "Is Leroy here?"

"He just left to pick up Lincoln from school." Lana looked at Charlie. "Lincoln goes to the Raymond Academy in Linden."

Charlie had heard of the exclusive private school located in a small town just north of Cotter Creek. Tuition was expensive, especially for parents working as a housekeeper and a gardener.

On the end table next to him, he noticed the picture of a young boy. He picked it up and looked at it. The dark-haired boy looked nothing like his red-haired mother. "Nice-looking boy," he commented, and put the picture back where it belonged.

"He's a good boy," Lana said, pride shining in her brown eyes. "He's smart as a whip and never gives us a minute of trouble."

"Must be tough paying to send him to the Raymond Academy," Charlie observed.

"It is, but Leroy and I agreed early on that we'd

make whatever sacrifices necessary to see that he gets the best education possible." She twisted the tissue in her lap. "Although with William gone, it looks like both of us are going to be without jobs, so I don't know how we'll manage Lincoln's school costs."

"I'd like to talk to you about William and Hope," Grace said. "You know Hope is in the hospital—that the sheriff believes she killed William and then took some sort of drug to knock herself unconscious?"

"That's nonsense. I spoke to Zack West and told him it was ridiculous to think that Hope would do such a thing. She's a sweet child and couldn't possibly do something like this. Did Hope and William argue? Absolutely. She's a teenager and that's what they do, but there's no way anyone will make me believe she killed him."

"Then that makes two of us," Grace said with fervor. It was obvious that Lana's words completely banished whatever momentary doubt had gripped her while in Hope's bedroom.

"Do you know of anyone William was having problems with?" Charlie asked. "A neighbor? A business associate? Anyone?"

Lana shook her head. "Believe me, I've racked my brain ever since I found him dead in his bed." Again a veil of tears misted her eyes.

"I can't think of anyone. He was a wonderful and gentle man. He was so good to me. One time, before I was married to Leroy, I wasn't feeling very well. I called William and told him I thought I had the flu and shouldn't come cook dinner for him. He showed up on my doorstep thirty minutes later with a pot of chicken soup he'd bought at the café. That's the kind of man he was. Who would want to kill a man like that?"

"That's what we're going to try to find out," Charlie said. He stood and pulled a business card from his back pocket. "If you think of anything that might help our defense of Hope, would you please give me a call?" He handed the card to Lana.

At that moment the front door opened, and Leroy and Lincoln came in. After Lana made the introductions, she told Lincoln to go to his room and do his homework.

As the well-mannered young boy disappeared into the back of the house, Charlie felt the chime of a biological clock he didn't know men possessed.

Since moving back to the family ranch in Cotter Creek, he'd been thinking about kids and recognizing that if he intended to start a family, it should be soon. He wasn't getting any younger.

Charlie sat down and turned his attention to Leroy. He was a big, burly man with a sun-darkened face and arms. His face seemed better suited for prize fighting, but at the moment his rough-hewn features held nothing but concern for his wife.

Leroy sat next to her and put an arm around her shoulder, as if to shield her from any unpleasantness.

Charlie asked Leroy the same questions he'd asked Lana and got no different answers. Leroy talked about what a wonderful man William had been and how he'd even helped pay for their wedding.

"I wish to God I knew who was responsible for this," Leroy said, his blunt features twisted with pain. "But, like we told the sheriff, we don't have a clue."

"We appreciate your time," Charlie said, recognizing that nothing more could be learned here. Once again he stood, and Grace followed suit.

"Grace?" Lana looked decidedly uncomfortable. "I know this probably isn't the time or the place, but Leroy and I don't know what we're supposed to do. Should we move out of here?"

Grace frowned thoughtfully. "I wouldn't do anything right now. We'll see what's going to happen with the estate. I'll check into it and let you know what's going on. Although I think Leroy should keep up the grounds, I'd prefer you stay out of the house for the time being." She took Lana's hand and smiled. "Consider yourself on paid vacation at the moment."

They all said their goodbyes, then Charlie and Grace left. "They must be terrified, not knowing what will happen to them now that William is gone," Grace said, as they walked back to the car.

"You should probably talk to William's attorney and find out about his will. Maybe he made some kind of provisions for them in the event of his death."

"His attorney is in Oklahoma City. I wonder if anyone has told him William is dead."

"I'll check with Zack," Charlie said. "And you might think about making funeral plans."

He could tell by the look on her face that she hadn't thought of that. "Oh God. I've been so overwhelmed. Of course, I need to take care of it." She looked stricken by the fact that she hadn't thought about it. "I'll speak with Mr. Burkwell tomorrow to find out what needs to be done." Jonathon Burkwell owned the Burkwell Funeral Home, the only such establishment in the town of Cotter Creek.

When they got to the car, Grace slid into the passenger seat and Charlie got behind the wheel. He started the engine, but then turned to look at her. "Have you called your mother, Grace? Maybe she should come help you take care of things."

Before replying, she averted her gaze and stared out the window. "No, there's no point in contacting her. She's out of the country, and there's really nothing she can do here. I'll be fine without her. Hope and I will be fine."

He studied her pretty profile. As a criminal defense attorney, Charlie was accustomed to people deceiving him, and he knew all the subtle signs of a liar. Right now he had the distinct feeling that Grace was lying to him about her mother.

It had been a day from hell. Grace sat at her desk in the back of the dress shop finishing up the payroll checks. The store had closed at seven, but on the night before payday she always stayed late in case any employees wanted to pick up their checks early.

She didn't mind staying. She was reluctant to go home and face the emptiness of her house and the tumultuous emotions that had been boiling inside her all day.

She'd spoken with William's attorney first thing that morning. He hadn't heard about the murder and was shocked. He, in turn, surprised Grace—she and Hope were the sole beneficiaries to William's fortune. Grace only hoped that fact didn't add to the body of evidence building against her sister.

The rest of the morning was spent making the necessary arrangements at Burkwell's funeral home. It was one of the most difficult things she'd ever done.

At noon, she and Charlie had taken the clothes and personal items to Hope. Grace visited with her sister while Charlie went to the cafeteria for a cup of coffee.

After the hospital visit, they'd gone back to the Covington mansion, where she went through William's desk, seeking something that might tell them who would have wanted him dead.

She still hadn't made herself open the door to William's room—the place where he had died—although she knew eventually she'd want to search it for anything that might help build a defense case for Hope.

She'd returned to the store at three-thirty, and now it was almost eight. She was exhausted but made no move to head home.

She'd just finished writing the last check when she heard the faint whoosh of the store door opening. "Grace?" a familiar voice called.

Grace jumped up from the desk and hurried out of her office. Standing just inside the door, with an eight-month-old baby boy on her hip, was Rachel Prescott, Grace's best friend.

"Oh honey, I just heard the news." Rachel approached her with a wrinkle of concern dancing across her forehead. "Jim had a three-day conference in Dallas, and I decided to go with him. We just got home a little while ago. How are you doing?"

"I'm okay. At least I'm trying to be okay." Grace smiled at the baby boy, who gave her a sleepy smile in return, then leaned his head against his mother's chest. "How's my Bobby?" She reached out and stroked his silky dark hair.

"He's pooped. He didn't have his nap today. So, tell me, what's this I hear about Hope being a suspect?"

"The medical examiner determined that William was killed between six and ten in the morning. Hope was the only one home. There were no signs of forced entry, and the murder weapon was found in Hope's hand." As Grace ticked off the pertinent points, a wave of discouragement swept over her.

Rachel laid a gentle hand on Grace's shoulder. "Sounds bad, but we both know Hope isn't capable of killing anybody." Grace smiled gratefully.

"I also heard you've hooked up with Charlie Black again," Rachel added, a hint of disapproval in her voice.

"Not hooked up as in 'hooked up,' I've just hired him to investigate the murder, and if the world goes crazy and Hope is arrested, I want him to defend her."

Rachel raised an eyebrow. "And who is defending you from Charlie?"

Rachel was the only person who knew the truth about how Charlie had broken Grace's heart, and she'd proclaimed him the most black-hearted, vile man on the face of the planet. At the time, Grace had relished her friend's anger on her behalf.

"Don't worry, I have no intention of making the same mistakes where Charlie is concerned. I just need him right now. He's good at what he does, but that doesn't mean I want him in my life on a personal level. I haven't forgotten, and I certainly haven't forgiven him."

Unfortunately, that didn't mean she didn't want him on some insane level. Over the last couple of days, she'd realized there was a part of her that had never really gotten over him.

"I just don't want to see you hurt again," Rachel said. "It's bad enough that you haven't dated since the breakup."

"That has nothing to do with him," Grace protested. "You know how busy I've been here at the shop."

"I know this place has become the perfect excuse for you," Rachel replied dryly.

Grace didn't respond. She couldn't exactly argue the point because she knew there was more than a kernel of truth to Rachel's words.

"Take that baby home and put him to bed," she finally said.

"Is there anything I can do? Any way I can help?" Rachel asked.

"Just pray they find the guilty party and that they don't arrest my sister," Grace replied. At that moment, the door to the shop opened once again, and one of her young, part-time employees came in to get her paycheck.

When Rachel and Bobby left, Grace gave the high school girl her check and then returned to her desk in the back room. She'd give it another half an hour or so before locking up the store and going home.

She kicked off her shoes beneath the desk and reached for the mug that held the last of the lukewarm coffee she'd been drinking all evening.

Charlie. Drat the man for being as attractive as he'd been eighteen months ago. From all indications, he appeared to have settled into ranching and small-town life with his usual aplomb.

The hard edge he'd possessed before seemed to be missing. He was still strong and self-assured, but he somehow seemed a bit more sensitive than he'd been during their six months together.

Not that it mattered. The familiar saying flitted through her mind: *Screw me once, shame on you. Screw me twice, shame on me.* She would be a fool to allow Charlie back into her heart in any way, shape or form. Charlie had proven himself unable to keep his pants on around other women.

Her present attraction to him was surely just due to her belief that he could save her sister and somehow make sense of the senseless.

She closed her business checkbook and locked it in the bottom desk drawer. Time to go home. Maybe tonight she would sleep without nightmares.

Maybe tonight visions of a blood-covered, knife-wielding Hope wouldn't haunt her. Maybe images of a dead William wouldn't visit her dreams.

Once again she heard the *whoosh* of the shop door opening. She quickly unlocked the desk drawer, pulled out the checkbook and then walked in her stocking feet from the office into the other room.

"Hello?" She frowned as she looked around the room. It was dimly lit with only a few security lights on, and she didn't see anyone inside.

Odd, she could have sworn she'd heard the front door open. Maybe she'd just imagined it. She glanced around one last time, then returned to her office, sat back in her chair, put the checkbook away and locked the drawer.

She moved her feet beneath the desk, seeking the shoes she'd kicked off minutes before. Suddenly Grace was eager to get home to the two-bedroom house she rented. She'd lived there for the past five years, long enough to fill it with her favorite colors and fabrics and make it a home where she enjoyed spending time.

Successful in finding her shoes, she stood and stretched with arms overhead, grateful that this trying day was finally at an end. Maybe tomorrow won't be so difficult. One could hope, she thought.

She grabbed her purse, turned off the office light and stepped out. Just as she was about to head for the front door, she felt a stir in the air and saw in her peripheral vision a ruffling of the dresses hanging on the rack.

"Hello? Is somebody here?" Her heartbeat quickened, and she gripped her purse handle. "Who's there?"

A dark shadow with a bat or length of pipe raised over his head exploded out of the clothes rack. He didn't make a sound, and the scream that rose up in the back of Grace's throat refused to release itself as she threw her purse at him and turned to run back to the office.

A lock. There was a lock on the office door. The words thundered through her brain as her heart threatened to burst out of her chest.

She had no idea who he was or what he wanted, but she didn't intend to stick around and ask questions. She ran past a mannequin and knocked it over, hoping to block his attack and gain an extra second or two to reach the office.

The mannequin banged to the floor, and she heard a hissed curse. Deep. Male. Oh God, what was he doing in here? What did he want?

She gasped as she reached the office door, but before she could grab the knob and turn it, something hard crashed into the back of her head. She crumpled to her knees as shooting stars went off in her brain.

The intruder kicked her twice in the ribs and frantic thoughts raced through her scrambled brain as she struggled to regain her breath. She knew if she didn't do something he was going to kill her.

"Grace?" The familiar female voice came from the front door, although to Grace it sounded as if it came from miles away. "Grace, are you here?"

It was only then that the scream that had been trapped inside her released itself. The attacker froze, then raced for the back door of the store. As he went through it, the alarm began to ring. The loud, buzzing noise was the last sound Grace heard as she gave in to the shooting stars and lost consciousness.

Chapter 5

Charlie stepped on the gas, breaking every speed limit in the state of Oklahoma as he raced toward the hospital. His heart beat so hard he felt nauseous and every nerve ending he possessed screamed in alarm.

He'd called Grace at home to make arrangements for meeting the next day, and when he didn't get her there, he'd tried Sophisticated Lady to see if she was working late. Deputy Ben Taylor answered and told him there'd been an attempted robbery at the store and that Grace had been transported to the hospital. He had no information on her condition, and Charlie jumped into his car almost before he could hang up the phone.

Now he squealed into the hospital lot and parked, his heart still pounding the rhythm of alarm. How badly had she been hurt? Had they caught the person who had broken in?

He raced into the ER and nearly ran into Zack coming out. He grabbed the man by his broad shoulders. "What happened? Where's Grace? Is she all right?"

Zack held up his hands. "Calm down, Charlie. She's going to be fine. She's got some bruised ribs and a possible concussion."

Charlie's heart dropped to his toes as he released his hold on Zack. "And you call that fine? Ben Taylor said something about a robbery at the store."

"We think that's what it was, but he was interrupted by Ben's wife showing up to get her paycheck. I've got to get back to the store, but if you want to see Grace, she's in examination room two."

Charlie hurried down the hallway, his hands clenching and unclenching. Bruised ribs? A possible concussion?

A simmering rage began to burn in his stomach as he thought of somebody hurting Grace. He hoped to hell Zack would find out who was responsible.

Charlie wasn't a violent man. He was accustomed to using his brain and mouth to solve fights, but at the moment, he wanted nothing more than to find the person who hurt Grace and beat the holy hell out of him.

The door to the examination room was closed. Charlie gave a soft knock but didn't wait for an answer before opening the door.

Clad in a worn, pale-blue-flowered hospital gown,

Grace sat on the edge of the examining-room table, her arms around her waist as the doctor sat in the chair before her.

Her eyes widened slightly at the sight of Charlie, and she winced as she shifted positions. "You didn't have to come here." Her normally strong voice was weak, reedy. The sound of it squeezed his heart.

"Of course I had to come here," he replied. "How is she?" He looked at the doctor, who wore a name tag that proclaimed him to be Dr. Devore.

"I have sore ribs and a headache. Other than that I'm fine," she answered. "In fact the doctor was just releasing me."

"Against my better judgment," Dr. Devore muttered beneath his breath. "She has quite a goose egg on the back of her head."

Charlie shot a look at Grace. She sighed and raised a trembling hand to her head. "He's worried that I might have a concussion and thinks I should spend the night."

."Then you should stay," Charlie said.

"I don't want to," she said crossly and dropped her hand from her head. "I'm a grown woman, Charlie. I know what's best for me, and I just need to go to bed. I'll be fine after a good night's sleep."

"If she goes home, somebody should stay with her throughout the night," Dr. Devore said, as he stood. "And if she suffers any nausea, vomiting or blurred vision, she needs to come right back in. I'll write you a pain prescription for your ribs, and the nurse will complete your discharge papers. Then I guess you can go."

"You aren't going home alone," Charlie said the moment the doctor left the room. "You have two choices, Grace. You can either have me as a house-guest for the night or you can come back to the ranch with me."

He saw the mutinous glare in her eyes and quickly continued, "Be reasonable, Grace. You shouldn't be alone. What if you get dizzy in the middle of the night and fall? What if you start throwing up and can't stop? Somebody needs to be with you."

"I don't want you in my house," she said hesitantly.

"Then come to mine," he replied. "I have a comfortable guest room, and if you're worried about being alone with me, don't be. Rosa will be there."

Once again she raised a hand to her head and winced. "Okay, I'll go to your place."

Her relatively easy capitulation surprised him and made him wonder just what had happened tonight in the shop and what was going on in her head. He intended to find out before the night was over.

"Can you take me by my house to get a few things?" she asked.

"Absolutely."

The nurse came in with her prescription and discharge papers. She reminded them of all the signs to watch for and to return to the emergency room should Grace experience anything unusual.

Charlie stepped out of the room so Grace could

get dressed, and while he waited for her he called Rosa to make sure she had the guest room ready.

When Grace opened the door of the examining room and stepped out, Charlie wanted to wrap her in his arms, hold her tight and make sure that nobody else ever hurt her again.

She was in obvious pain as they walked to his car, and once again rage coupled with fierce protectiveness filled him.

Their first stop was at the pharmacy, where they filled the prescription for her pain pills. He wanted her to wait in the car while he ran in, but she insisted on going in.

From the drugstore, he drove to her house. He'd never been inside it before. Their dates had usually taken place in Oklahoma City when she was there on business.

They'd had two dates here in Cotter Creek when he'd come back to visit his father, and it had been on those dates he'd met Hope, but he'd never been invited into her personal space.

As he stepped into her living room, two things struck him: the lime and lavender color scheme that was both soothing and sensual, and the magnificent scent of jasmine and vanilla that lingered in the air.

When Grace disappeared down the hallway to her bedroom, he walked around the living room, taking in the furnishings and knickknacks that showed the nuances of her personality.

The sofa looked elegant yet comfortable, and the

bookshelf held an array of paperback books and framed photos of both Hope and William. What was curiously missing were any photos of her mother. Again Charlie wondered about the whereabouts of the elusive Elizabeth Covington and the relationship she had with her daughters.

Right now, what he really wanted to know was what Grace's bedroom looked like. Was her bed covered with luxurious silk sheets that smelled like her? Did she still own that sexy little red nightgown that hugged her curves and exposed just enough skin to make his mind go blank?

He sat on the sofa and mentally chastised himself. He had to stop thinking about things like that—had to stop torturing himself with memories of how her long hair had felt splayed across his bare chest and how she loved to cuddle and run her finger through his thatch of chest hair.

He remembered the two of them running naked into his kitchen to bake a frozen pizza after a bout of hot, wild sex, slow-dancing on his balcony and the philosophical debates that usually ended in laughter.

She was smart and sexy—everything he'd wanted in a woman—but he'd thought she was playing for fun and hadn't realized she was playing for keeps. She'd breezed into his life every weekend or so. She hadn't been inclined to share much information about her personal life. Instead they had spent their time together living in the moment.

Now, as he sat on the sofa with those old regrets weighing heavy, he realized that despite their intense relationship there were many things he didn't know about her, many things they hadn't shared.

He stood up when she returned to the living room with a small, flowery overnight bag in her hand. He took the bag from her, and moments later they were in his car, headed toward his ranch.

"You want to tell me exactly what happened tonight?" he asked.

"I figured you already knew. Somebody tried to rob the store."

He glanced at her. She was ghostly pale in the light from the dashboard. "That's the short version. I want all the details," he said gently.

She leaned her head back against the seat, winced slightly and closed her eyes. "I was in the back in the office and went out to greet whoever had come in, but I didn't see anyone so I went back to the office to lock up my desk and get ready to leave. I was halfway to the front door when he came out of the rack of clothes."

Charlie's hands tightened around the steering wheel as he heard the slight tremor in her voice and felt her fear grow palpable in the car.

"And then what?" he asked.

"He had a bat or something like that in his hands. I ran back toward the office. I knew if I could get inside I could lock the door and call for help." She drew a tremulous breath. "I almost made it." She opened her eyes and gave him a wry smile. "I guess I shouldn't have stopped to admire that cute blouse on the mannequin."

Her smile began to tremble and fell away as tears filled her eyes. "I'd just reached the office door when he hit me in the back of the head. I fell to my knees and he started to kick me." A small sob escaped her, but she quickly sucked in a breath to stop her tears. "If Dana hadn't come in for her paycheck, I don't know what would have happened."

"You didn't see who it was? You couldn't make an identification?"

"No. All I saw was a big, dark shadow." She sucked in another breath and wiped her eyes before the tears could fall. "I guess I should be grateful that he didn't get the money in the cash register." Once again she leaned her head back and closed her eyes.

Charlie said nothing, but his blood ran cold. What kind of a robber would walk right past the cash register and hide in a rack of clothes? If he'd truly been after quick cash, why not take the money from the register and escape out the front door?

His hands clenched tighter on the steering wheel as alarms rang in his head. What she'd just described didn't sound like an attempted robbery. It sounded like attempted murder.

Under any other circumstances, Grace would have never agreed to go to Charlie's for the night, but the truth was that she was afraid to be alone. The attack had shaken her up more than she wanted to admit, and even now as she closed her eyes, all she could see was a vision of the big shadow leaping out at her.

Almost as upsetting as the attack itself was the fact that she couldn't think of a single friend who would welcome her into their home. Over the last couple of years she'd been so focused on the store, she hadn't taken the time to nurture friendships. Her relationship with Rachel was the only one she'd managed to maintain, and she was reluctant to barge into Rachel's happy home where she lived with her adoring husband and baby boy.

With William gone and Hope in the hospital, she really had no place else to turn but to Charlie. At least Rosa would be there.

A surge of anger swelled up inside Grace. Her mother should be here. Her mother should be the person calming her fears, offering her support and comfort. The anger was short-lived. She was unable to sustain it as her head pounded and her ribs ached.

She was grateful when Charlie pulled up to the ranch. Lights blazed from almost every window. All she wanted was a pain pill and a bed where she'd feel safe for the remainder of the night.

Rosa greeted them at the front door, fussing like a mother hen as she led Grace to the airy, open kitchen. "I'm going to make you a nice hot cup of tea, then it's bed for you, you poor thing."

As Grace eased down into a chair at the table and Charlie sat across from her, Rosa bustled around, preparing the tea. Despite the pounding of her head, Grace found the hominess of the room comforting. Maybe a cup of tea would banish the icy knot inside her chest.

It smelled like apple pie spices, and a vase of

fresh-cut daisies sat in the center of the round oak table. The yellow gingham curtains added a dash of cheer.

"Tell me again what happened," Charlie said.

"She will not," Rosa said, her plump face wrinkling in disapproval as she shot a stern look at him. "There will be time for you to talk tomorrow. Right now what she needs is to drink that tea and get into bed. Haven't you noticed that she's pale as a ghost and in obvious pain?"

Grace looked at Charlie, and in the depths of his gray eyes, she saw compassion and caring and a flicker of something else, something deeper that both scared her and sent a rumbling shock wave through her.

She quickly broke eye contact with him and stared into her cup. Coming here had been a mistake. She didn't want to see Charlie here in his home environment, one so different from his apartment in Oklahoma City.

"You want one of those pills?" Charlie asked.

She nodded. "I'd like a handful, but I'll settle for one."

"Your head still hurt?" he asked, as he got the bottle and shook out one of the pills.

"The only thing that takes my mind off how bad my head hurts is the pain in my ribs." She forced a small smile that turned into a wince.

"I'm just going to go turn down your bed and fluff your pillows," Rosa said, and left the kitchen.

Grace took the pill and sipped her tea, the warmth working its way into icy territory. She'd been cold since the moment the attacker had leapt out of the clothes rack. She would have given him any money she had if he'd demanded it. He hadn't needed to hit her over the head and kick her.

She was aware of Charlie's gaze on her, intent and somber. "What?" she finally asked. "What are you thinking, Charlie?"

"I'm thinking maybe we have a lot to talk about tomorrow."

Instinctively she knew he was talking about more than William's murder case, about more than the attack on her tonight. She frowned.

"Charlie, if you think I'm going to talk about anything that happened before three days ago, then you're wrong. I have no desire to go back and hash out our past. I told you what I want from you. I want you to keep Hope out of jail. I appreciate what you're doing for me tonight, but don't mistake my need for your abilities as an attorney and investigator for a need for anything else. Don't mistake my gratitude for anything other than that."

Her speech exhausted her. Thankfully at that moment Rosa returned to the kitchen and Grace stood, a bit unsteady on her feet.

Charlie was at her side in an instant, his arm under hers for support. "Let's get you into bed," he said.

She was already feeling the initial effect of the pain medication, a floating sensation that took the edge off and made her legs a bit wobbly. She rarely took any kind of pain meds. She hated the feeling of being even slightly out of control.

Charlie led her down the hallway, and for a single, crazy moment, she wished he were going to crawl into bed with her. Not for sex—although sex with Charlie had always been amazing.

No, what she yearned for was his big, strong arms around her. He'd always been a great cuddle partner, and she'd never felt as loved, as safe, as when she'd been snuggled against him with his arms wrapped around her.

"You should be okay in here," he said as they stepped into the room.

The guest room was large and decorated in various shades of blue. The bed was king-sized, the bedspread turned down to reveal crisp, white sheets.

"Do you want me to send in Rosa to help you get into your nightclothes?" he asked.

"No, I'll be fine," she replied. Her voice seemed to come from someplace far away. She looked up at him, his face slightly blurry, and again she was struck by a desire to fall into his arms—to burrow her head against his strong chest and let him hold her through the night.

"You need to go now, Charlie," she said, and pushed him away.

He stepped back toward the door. "You'll let me know if you need anything?"

"You'll be the first to know."

He turned to leave but then faced her once again. "Grace? I could kill the man who did this to you." His deep voice rumbled and his eyes flashed darkly.

She sat on the edge of the bed. "I appreciate the sentiment," she said. "Good night, Charlie."

"'Night, Grace." He closed the door, and she was alone in the room.

It took what seemed like forever to get out of her clothes and into her nightgown. She went into the adjoining bathroom and brushed her teeth, then returned to the bedroom, where she turned out the bedside lamp and fell into bed.

It was only when she was finally alone that she began to cry. She didn't know if her tears were for William, for Hope, for her mother or for herself.

And she feared they just might be tears because, in the past, Charlie Black hadn't been the man she'd thought he was, the man she'd wanted him to be.

Chapter 6

It was just after two in the morning, and Charlie sat in the recliner chair by the window in the living room, staring out at the moonlit night.

He'd grown up on the ranch, and some of his happiest memories were of things that occurred here. He'd loved the feel of a horse beneath him and the smell of the rich earth, but in college, his head had gotten twisted, and suddenly the ranch hadn't seemed good enough for him.

He'd been a fool. A shallow, stupid fool.

A year ago he would have never dreamed that he'd be back here on the ranch. He'd been living in the fast lane, making more money than he'd ever dreamed possible and enjoying a lifestyle of excess.

Meeting Grace had been the icing on the cake. He'd eagerly looked forward to the two weekends a month she came into town and stayed with him. Although he would have liked more from her, he got the feeling from her that he was an indulgence, like eating ice cream twice a month. But nobody really wanted a steady diet of ice cream.

He'd thought he was her boy toy. They'd never spoken about their relationship, never laid down ground rules or speculated on where it was going. They'd just enjoyed it.

Until that night. That crazy Friday night when things—when *he*—had spiraled out of control.

He shoved these thoughts from his mind and closed his eyes and drew a weary breath. He was tired, but sleep remained elusive. The attack on her earlier tonight worried him because it didn't make sense.

If the goal of the person in the store had been to rob it, then why carry in a bat, why not a gun? Why leave the cash register untouched and go after Grace? Had he thought that her cash might be locked away in the office? Possibly.

He sat up straighter in his chair as he sensed movement in the hallway. He reached over and turned on the small lamp on the table next to his chair.

Grace appeared in the doorway. She was wearing a short, pink silk robe tied around her slender waist, and her hair was tousled from sleep. She didn't appear to be surprised that he was still awake.

"Can't sleep?" he asked.

"I had a bad dream. I tried to go back to sleep, but decided maybe it was time for another pain pill." She walked across the room to the sofa and curled up with her bare legs beneath her. "What's your excuse for being up this time of the night?"

"No bad dreams, just confusing thoughts."

"What kind of confusing thoughts?" she asked, and then held up a hand. "Wait, I don't want to know, at least not tonight." She reached up and smoothed a strand of her golden hair away from her face. "Talk to me about pleasant things, Charlie. I feel like the last couple of days have been nothing but bad things. Tell me about your life here at the ranch. What made you decide to move back here?"

"You heard about Dad's heart attack?"

She nodded. "And I'm sorry."

"Initially I was just going to come back here to deal with whatever needed to be taken care of to get the place on the market and sold, but something happened in those days right after I buried Dad."

He paused a moment and stared back out the window, but it was impossible to see anything but his own reflection. In truth, his life had begun a transformation on the night that Grace left him, but he knew she wouldn't want to hear that, probably wouldn't believe him, anyway.

He looked back at her. "I realized that I hated my life, that I missed waking up in the mornings and hearing the cows lowing in the pasture, that I missed the feel of a horse beneath me and the warm sun on my back. I realized it was time to come home to Cotter Creek."

She leaned her head back against the cushions. "When I was planning to open a dress shop, William told me I could use the money he loaned me to open one anywhere in the country, but it never entered my mind to be anywhere but here," she said. "Cotter Creek is and always will be home. I love it here, the small-town feel, the people, everything. Has the transition been tough for you?"

"Learning the ins and outs of ranching has been challenging," he admitted. "Even though I grew up here I never paid much attention to the day-to-day details. I already had my sights set on something different than the ranch. My ranch hands have had a fine time tormenting the city boy in me. The first thing they told me was that cow manure was a natural cleaner for Italian leather shoes."

She laughed and that's exactly what he'd wanted, to hear that rich, melodic sound coming from her. She was a woman made for laughter, and for the next few minutes he continued to tell her about the silly things that had happened when he'd first taken over the ranch.

He embellished each story as necessary to get the best entertainment value—needing, wanting, to keep her laughing so the dark shadows of fear and worry wouldn't claim her eyes again.

"Stop," she finally said, her arms wrapped around her ribs.

"You need that pain pill now?" he asked.

"No, I don't think so. To be honest, what I'd like

is something to eat. Maybe I could just fix a quick sandwich or something. I didn't eat dinner last night," she said with a touch of apology.

"I'll bet there's some leftover roast beef from Rosa's dinner in the fridge. Want to come into the kitchen or do you want me to fix you a plate and bring it to you?"

She unfolded those long, shapely legs of hers. "I'll come to the kitchen." She stood and frowned. "We won't wake up Rosa, will we?"

"Nah. First of all she sleeps like the dead, and secondly her room is on the other side of the house." Charlie got up and followed her into the kitchen, trying not to notice how the silky robe clung to her lush curves.

He flipped on the kitchen light, and as she slid into a chair at the table, he walked over to the refrigerator, then turned back to look at her. "If you'd rather not have leftover roast, I could whip up an omelet with toast."

She looked at him in surprise. "You never used to cook."

He knew she was remembering that when they had been seeing each other he'd always taken his meals out, keeping only prepared food in his apartment that required nothing more than opening a lid or popping it into the microwave.

"When I came back here to the ranch, I learned survival cooking skills. Rosa takes three days off a week to stay with her son and his family, and during those days I'm on my own. So, cooking became a necessity, and to my surprise I rather like it."

"The roast beef is fine," she replied.

He felt her gaze lingering on him as he got out the leftover meat and potatoes and arranged them on a plate, then ladled gravy over everything and popped it into the microwave.

Was she remembering those midnight raids they'd made on his refrigerator after making love? When they'd eat cold chicken with their fingers or eat ice cream out of the carton?

Did she remember anything good about their time together, or had his betrayal left only the bad times in her head?

"Are you dating, Grace? Got a special fella in your life?" he asked.

She raised a perfectly arched blond eyebrow. "If I had somebody special in my life, I wouldn't be sitting here now," she replied, confirming what he'd already assumed. "I've been too busy at the shop to date, besides the fact that I'm just not interested in a relationship."

The microwave dinged and Charlie turned around to retrieve the food. He wanted to ask her if he was responsible for the fact that she didn't want a relationship, if he'd left such a bad mark on her heart that she wasn't interested in ever pursuing a relationship again. If that was the case, it would be tragic.

He placed the steaming plate before her, got her a glass of milk and sat across from her as she began to eat.

"What about you?" she asked between bites. "Are you dating somebody here in town? I'm sure there were plenty of fluttering hearts when the news got out that you had moved back."

"I would venture a guess that yours wasn't one of those that fluttered?"

She raised that dainty eyebrow again. "That would be a good guess," she replied.

He leaned back in his chair and shook his head. "I'm not seeing anyone, haven't for quite some time. Apparently Dad hadn't been feeling well for a while before his death, and the ranch had kind of gotten away from him. I've been incredibly busy since I moved back. I haven't had the time or the inclination to date."

"Charlie Black too busy for fun? Hold the presses!" she exclaimed.

He gazed at her for a long moment. "You've got to stop that, Grace," he finally said. "If you want my continued help, you need to stop with the not-so-subtle digs. I understand how you feel about me. You don't have to remind me with sarcastic cuts."

She held his gaze as a tinge of pink filled her cheeks. "You're right, I'm sorry." She turned her attention to her plate and set her fork down. "I'm just so filled with anger right now and you're an easy target."

He leaned forward and covered her hand with his, surprised when she didn't pull away from him. "We'll sort this all out, Grace. I promise you."

She surprised him further by turning her hand over and entwining her fingers with his. "I hope so. Right now everything just seems like such a mess."

"It is a mess," he agreed. "But messes can be

cleaned up." Except the one he'd made with her, he reminded himself.

She let go of his hand and picked up her fork once again. As she continued to eat, Charlie once again spoke of ranch life, trying to keep the conversation light and easy.

When she was finished eating, she started to get up to take her plate to the sink, but he stopped her and instead grabbed the dish himself.

"I'm not used to somebody waiting on me," she said.

"You never struck me as a woman who wanted or needed anyone to wait on you," he replied, as he rinsed the dishes and stuck them in the dishwasher. "One of your strengths is that you're self-reliant and independent. And one of your weaknesses is that you're self-reliant and independent." He smiled and pointed a finger at her. "And no, that doesn't open the door for you to point out all my weaknesses."

She laughed, then reached up and touched her temple. "Now I think I'm ready for a pain pill and some more sleep."

When she got up from the table, Charlie tried un-successfully not to notice that her robe had come untied. As she stood, he caught a glimpse of the curve of her creamy breast just above the neckline of the pink nightgown she wore beneath.

Desire jolted through him, stunning him with the force of it. Maybe this was his penance, he thought, as he followed her out of the kitchen. Fate had forced them together, and his punishment was to want her forever and never have the satisfaction of possessing her again.

As they passed through the living room, he turned out the lamp, knowing that if he didn't get some sleep tonight he wouldn't be worth a plugged nickel the next day.

When they reached the door to her room, she turned and looked at him. Her gaze seemed softer than it had since the moment she'd pulled up in her convertible and demanded his help.

"Thank you, Charlie, for feeding me and letting me stay here tonight. I really appreciate everything." She reached up and placed her palm on the side of his cheek, and he fought the impulse to turn his face into her touch. "Part of you is such a good man."

She dropped her hand to her side. "I just wish I could forgive and forget the parts of you that aren't such a good man."

She turned and went into the bedroom, closing the door firmly in his face.

Grace woke with the sun slashing through the gauzy curtains and the sound of horse hooves someplace in the distance. She remained in bed, thinking about her life, about what lay ahead and, finally, about Charlie.

Funny that the man who had hurt her more than any man in her life was also the one who made her feel the most safe. She'd slept without worry, comforted by the fact that Charlie was in the room across the hall.

Surely it was just because of all that had happened, that she'd so easily let him back in her life.

She was off-kilter, careening around in a landscape that was utterly foreign to her. Was it any wonder she'd cling to the one person she'd thought she'd known better than anyone else in the world?

With a low moan, she finally pulled herself to a sitting position on the side of the bed. She'd felt awful the night before, and although her head had stopped pounding, her body felt as if it had been contorted in positions previously unknown to the human body.

Her ribs were sore, but not intolerably so. No more pain pills, she told herself, as she headed for the bathroom. What she needed was a hot shower to loosen her muscles and clear her head. Then she needed to get Charlie to take her home.

Before falling asleep last night, she'd come to the conclusion that the attack in the shop had been an attempted robbery. It was the only thing that made sense.

The robber had obviously thought there was nothing in the register and probably assumed she had a safe or a cash box in the office. He probably wouldn't have attacked her at all if she'd gone directly to the front door and left instead of noticing the sway of the clothes on the rack in front of his hiding place. She went to the bathroom and turned on the shower.

She'd never felt such terror as when he'd jumped out of the clothes rack and raced toward her, the long object held over his head. If he'd hit her just a little harder, he could have bashed her skull in and killed her.

Shivering, she quickly stepped beneath the hot spray of water, needing the warmth to cast away the chill her thought evoked.

The shower did help, although her ribs still ached when she drew a deep breath or moved too fast. She dressed in the jeans and blouse she'd packed in her overnight bag, then left the bedroom in search of Charlie.

She found Rosa in the kitchen by herself. The plump woman sat at the table with a cup of coffee in front of her. When she saw Grace, she jumped to her feet with surprising agility.

"Sit," Grace exclaimed. "Just point me to the cabinet with the cups. I can get my own coffee."

"What about breakfast?" Rosa asked, as she pointed a finger to the cabinet next to the sink. "You should eat something."

"Nothing for me. I'm fine. I had some of your roast beef at about three this morning. It was delicious, by the way." Grace poured herself a cup of the coffee and joined the housekeeper at the table. "Where's Charlie?"

"Out riding the ranch. He should be back in a little while. How are you feeling this morning?"

"Sore, but better than last night." Grace took a sip of the coffee.

"Charlie was worried about you. I could see it in his eyes. He used to get that look when his mama was having bad days. She had cancer, you know. She was diagnosed when he was ten and didn't pass away until he was fourteen. Those four years were tough on him, but I'm sure you knew all that."

"Actually, I didn't," Grace replied. She'd known that Charlie's mother had passed away when he was a teenager, but that was all she'd known.

At that moment, the back door opened and he walked in, bringing with him that restless energy he possessed and the scent of sunshine and horseflesh. The smile he offered her shot a starburst of warmth through her.

"Grace, how are you feeling?" He shrugged out of a navy jacket and hung it on a hook near the backdoor, then walked to the cabinet and grabbed a cup.

"Better. A little sore, but I think I'm going to live." She didn't want to notice how utterly masculine he looked in his worn jeans and the white T-shirt that pulled taut across his broad shoulders. With his lean hips and muscled chest and arms, he definitely turned women's heads.

She'd always thought he was born to wear a suit— that elegant dress slacks and button-down shirts were made for him. But she'd been mistaken. He looked equally hot in his casual wear.

"I'm glad you're feeling better," he said, as he joined them at the table. "Did you get breakfast?"

"Said she didn't want any," Rosa replied.

"And I don't. What I'd like is for you to take me home now." She looked at Charlie expectantly.

He frowned and Rosa stood, looking from one to the other. "I'm going to go take care of some laundry," she said, and left the two of them alone at the table.

Charlie took a sip of his coffee, eyeing her over

the rim of the mug. "I wish you'd consider staying here for a couple more days," he said.

"There's no reason to do that. I'm feeling much better." She wrapped her fingers around her cup as his frown deepened.

"You might be feeling better, but I'm not. I don't like what happened to you last night, Grace."

She laughed. "I wasn't too excited about it, either, but it was an attempted robbery. It could have happened to anyone."

"But it didn't happen to anyone. It happened to you." His gaze held hers intently. "And given what happened to William, it just makes me nervous. It makes me damned nervous."

She leaned back in her chair and looked at him in surprise. "Surely you can't think that one thing had anything to do with the other?" she exclaimed. "You're overreacting, Charlie."

"Maybe," he agreed, and took another sip of his coffee.

"How can you possibly connect what happened to William to the attack on me at the store last night?"

"I can't right now." His lips were thin with tension. "But, I'd prefer we be too cautious than not cautious enough."

"Then I'll do things differently at the store. I realize now how incredibly stupid it was of me to leave the shop door unlocked when I was in the back room. Maybe whoever came in knew that it was payday and hoped I'd have some of the payroll in cash. I just can't believe it was anything other than that, and there's no reason for me to stay here another night."

She wasn't going to let him talk her into staying. Last night after he'd fixed her the meal and walked her back to the bedroom, she'd almost kissed him. When she'd placed her palm on the side of his face, she'd wanted to lean in and take his mouth with hers.

It had been an insane impulse, one that she was grateful she hadn't followed through on, but she felt the need to gain some distance from him.

There was no way she wanted to stay here another night with him. She was more than a little weak where he was concerned.

"I suppose you're going to be stubborn about this," he said.

"I suppose so," she agreed.

He drained his coffee cup and got up from the table. "Just let me take a quick shower and I'll take you home."

"Actually you can just drop me at the shop."

"You're actually planning to work today?" He raised an eyebrow in disapproval. "Don't you think it would be wise to give yourself a day of rest?" He carried his coffee cup to the sink.

"Actually, I think you're right. While you're showering, I'll make arrangements for somebody else to work both today and this evening. My ribs are still pretty sore, and I didn't get a lot of sleep last night. A day of lazing around sounds pretty good."

He nodded, as if satisfied with her answer. "Give

me fifteen, twenty minutes, then I'll be ready to take you to get your car."

As he left the kitchen, Grace sipped her coffee. Although she didn't want to admit it, there was a part of her that dreaded going back into the store, where last night she'd thought she was going to die.

She heard a phone ring someplace in the back of the house. It rang only once and then apparently was answered. It reminded her that she needed to make some calls.

She dug her cell phone out of her purse, grateful that Rosa had left it on the kitchen table where she would find it easily this morning. She made the calls to arrange for the shop to run smoothly without her today. Thankfully she had dependable and trustworthy employees to take over for her. She also needed to check on the final funeral arrangements for William.

When the calls were finished, she got up from the table and carried her cup to the sink, then went back to the bedroom to retrieve her overnight bag.

She could hear running water and knew Charlie was in the shower. She sat on the edge of the bed as memories swept over her—memories of hot, steaming water and Charlie gliding a bar of soap over her shoulders and down her back, of the feel of his soapy hands cupping her breasts, of his slick body pressed against her. More than once they'd left the shower stall, covered with suds and fallen into Charlie's king-sized bed to finish what they'd started.

She shook her head to dislodge the old images.

Rising from the bed, she grabbed her bag, then went back into the kitchen to wait for Charlie.

Grace pulled out her cell phone and called the hospital. "Hi, honey," she said when Hope's voice filled the line.

"Grace!" Hope instantly began to cry.

"Hope, what's wrong?" Grace squeezed the phone more tightly against her ear. "Honey, why are you crying? Has something happened?"

"I heard from a nurse this morning that something bad happened to you last night, that you were attacked. I thought I'd never see you again, that it would be just like Mom and you'd be gone forever."

Grace wished she could reach through the line and hug her sister. "I'm not going anywhere, Hope. You can always depend on me," she said fervently.

Again she mentally cursed her mother for abandoning them, for going away and leaving behind so many questions and so much pain.

"It was a robbery attempt, Hope, but I'm okay. I promise and we're going to be okay. You and I together, we're going to be just fine. We're going to get through all of this." She glanced up as Charlie entered the room, bringing with him the scent of minty soap and shaving cream. "I'll be in to see you sometime this morning, okay? You just hang in there. You have to be strong."

She hung up and stood to face Charlie. "I'm ready," she said.

"You'd better sit back down."

It was only then that she saw the darkness in his

eyes, the muscle working in his jaw. A screaming alarm went off inside her.

"Why? What's going on?" Her heart began to beat a frantic rhythm and her legs threatened to buckle as she sat once again.

"I got a call from Zack." He frowned, as if searching for words, which was ridiculous because Charlie was never at a loss for them. "Hope is being arrested this morning. She's going to be charged with first-degree murder."

Grace grabbed hold of the top of the table, her fingertips biting into the wood as his words reverberated through her head.

Chapter 7

If there was any chance of Charlie becoming a drinking man again, the events of the past three days certainly would have driven him to the bottle.

Hope had been arraigned on Tuesday morning in front of the toughest judge Charlie had ever butted heads against. The prosecuting attorney, up for reelection in the fall, had come with both barrels loaded. He'd suggested the judge send a message to the youth around the country, that no matter what the age or the circumstances, murder was never acceptable.

He'd requested no bail be set, and although Charlie had argued vigorously, nearly garnering himself a contempt charge, the judge had agreed with the prosecutor.

Hope would await trial at the Beacon Juvenile Detention Center in Oklahoma City. A plea deal had been offered to her. The authorities believed it was probable she hadn't acted alone, that it was her boyfriend, Justin, who actually killed William.

Hope refused to accept the deal, sticking to her story that she had no idea what had happened that morning at the house.

William's attorney had traveled to Cotter Creek and sat down with Charlie and Grace to go over the will. The estate had been left to Grace and Hope, with Grace as executor. He'd left some of his money to local charities and a generous amount to Lana for her years of service. He'd also left a small amount of money to Grace's mother.

After the meeting with the lawyer, they had visited with the Racines. Grace assured Lana and Leroy that she had no intention of selling the house anytime soon and would continue to pay their salaries if they wanted to stay on doing their usual duties. She also told them about the money William had left to Lana.

Hope's incarceration at the detention center was difficult for Grace, although as usual she kept a stiff upper lip and didn't display the emotions Charlie knew had to be boiling inside her.

Charlie now checked his watch with a frown. Time to leave. He was picking Grace up at ten for William's funeral. After the ceremony was over, they were driving into Oklahoma City to visit Hope. It was going to be a grim, long day.

He left the ranch and headed toward Grace's place. Charlie felt that tingle of excitement, a crazy swell of emotion in his chest—the same feeling he'd always gotten when he knew she was coming into Oklahoma City for the weekend. He would spend the entire week before filled with eager anticipation, half sick by wanting the days of the week to fly by quickly. By Saturday night, he'd be sick again, dreading the coming of Sunday when she'd return to Cotter Creek. He'd never asked her for more than what she gave him, was afraid that in asking he'd only push her away from him.

He shoved these thoughts out of his head as he pulled up in front of her house. She was waiting for him on the porch, a solitary woman in an elegant black dress. He got out of the car as she approached, and his heart squeezed at the dark, deep sadness in her eyes.

"Good morning," he said, as he opened the car door to let her in. "Are you ready for this?"

"I don't think you're ever ready for something like this," she replied.

He closed the door, went back around to the driver's seat and got in. "You look tired," he said, as he headed toward the cemetery. The wake had been the night before and was followed by an open house at Grace's place.

"After everyone left last night, I had trouble going to sleep," she said. "I'm sure I'll sleep better once the funeral is over and I get a chance to see that Hope's okay."

He nodded. "Zack turned over copies of William's financial records to me. I spent last night going through them looking for any anomalies that might raise a flag."

"Let me guess, you didn't find anything."

"Nothing that looked at all suspicious." He felt the weight of her gaze on him.

"We aren't doing very well at coming up with an alternate suspect," she observed.

"Unfortunately it isn't as easy as just pulling a name out of a hat. I intend to make a case that Justin is responsible."

"Then why hasn't he been arrested?" she asked. "Zack has made it pretty clear he thinks Justin was involved."

"Thinking and proving are two different things. Unfortunately Justin's roommate has provided him with an alibi for the time of the murder." His roommate, Sam Young, certainly was no paragon of virtue. Sam worked in a tattoo parlor and had a reputation for being a tough guy.

They fell silent for the rest of the drive to the cemetery. When they arrived, the parking lot was already filled with cars, indicating that there was a huge turnout of people to say goodbye to William Covington.

The Cotter Creek Cemetery was a pretty place, with plenty of old shade trees. Wilbur Cummins, the caretaker, took particular pride not only in maintaining the grounds but also in making sure that all the headstones were in good shape. A plethora of flowers filled the area.

As they waited for the ceremony to begin, people walked over to give their regards to Grace.

"I'm so sorry for your loss," Savannah West said, as she reached for Grace's hand. Savannah worked for the Cotter Creek newspaper and was married to one of the brothers who ran West Protective Services.

"Thanks." Grace turned and looked at Charlie. "Savannah is one of my best customers at the shop."

Savannah shoved a strand of wild red hair away from her face. "Still no arrest in the attempted robbery and assault?"

Grace shook her head. "I wasn't able to give Zack any kind of a description, so I'm not expecting any arrest."

"The criminals are running amuck in Cotter Creek. Zack is just sick about it and about what's happening with Hope," Savannah said.

Charlie felt the wave of Grace's despair as she nodded stiffly and her eyes grew glassy with tears. Savannah grabbed Grace's hand once again. "Zack was against making the arrest, but that ass of a prosecutor Alan Connor insisted."

"It doesn't matter," Charlie said. "Hope is innocent, and we'll prove it where it counts, in a court of law."

Grace placed a hand on his arm and smiled gratefully. Then it was time for the service to begin. As the preacher gave the eulogy, Charlie scanned the crowd.

Grace was right. Other than Justin, they hadn't managed to come up with a single lead that would point them away from Hope.

It was an eclectic crowd. Ranchers uncomfortable in their Sunday suits stood beside men Charlie didn't know, men who wore their expensive power suits with casual elegance. He assumed these were business associates of William's, and he noticed Zack West had those men in his sights as well.

Was it possible that William had been working on a business deal nobody knew about? Something that might have stirred up a motive for murder? At this point, he was willing to grasp at any alternative theory to Hope being a murderer.

Lana and Leroy Racine stood side by side, Leroy's big arm around his wife's shoulders as she wept uncontrollably. Certainly they had nothing to gain by William's death; rather, it was just the opposite. They stood to lose both their jobs and their home.

The only people who had a lot to gain by William's death were Grace and Hope, both of whom Charlie would have staked his life were innocent. But how had Hope gotten drugged? Who had managed to get into the house without breaking a window or a door? Who had killed William?

What he hoped was that Zack was doing his job and would give him a heads-up if he discovered any leads. Right now, coming up with a reasonable defense for Hope seemed impossible.

Grace remained stoic throughout the funeral, standing rigidly beside him. An island of strength, that was how he'd always thought of her. An island of a woman who took care of herself and her own needs, a woman who had never really needed him. And he was a man who needed to be needed.

When the ceremony was finally over and the final well-wishing had been given, most of the crowd headed for their cars, and Charlie gently took hold of Grace's arm.

"You ready to go?"

She nodded wearily. "I loved him, you know. He was as loving and kind a father as I could have ever asked for." She leaned into Charlie.

They were halfway to the car when a tall, gray-haired man who greeted Grace with a friendly smile stopped them. She introduced him as Hank Weatherford, William's closest neighbor.

"I was wondering if we could sit down together when you get a chance," Hank said. Grace looked at him with curiosity. He continued, "I've been trying to talk William into selling me the five acres of land between his place and mine. It's got nothing on it but weeds and an old shed. Now that he's gone I thought maybe you'd be agreeable to the idea."

Charlie narrowed his eyes as he stared at the older man. Interesting. A land dispute over five acres hardly seemed like a motive for murder, but Charlie smelled a contentious relationship between Hank Weatherford and William.

"Mr. Weatherford, I'll have to get back to you. I haven't decided yet what I'm going to do with the estate," Grace said.

He nodded. "Just keep in mind that I'd like to sit down and talk with you about those five acres."

"I'll keep it in mind," Grace agreed.

"That was interesting," Charlie said once he and Grace were in his car. "What's the deal with these five acres?"

"William always talked about having it cleaned up and maybe putting in a pool or a tennis court, but he never got around to it. I imagine Hank is tired of looking at the mess." She shot him a sharp glance. "Surely you don't think Hank had anything to do with William's death."

"Take nothing for granted, Grace. You'd be amazed at why people commit murder."

From the cemetery they went to her place, where they both changed clothes for the drive to Oklahoma City. Charlie had brought with him a pair of jeans and a short-sleeved light blue dress shirt, and he changed in her guest room.

She changed from her somber dress into a pair of jeans and a peach-colored blouse that enhanced the blue of her eyes and her blond coloring.

By one o'clock they were on the road. They hoped to get to the detention center by three, which would let them visit with Hope for an hour.

Grace seemed a million miles away as they drove. She stared out the window, not speaking, and she had a lost, uncertain look that was so unlike her, and it broke Charlie's heart just a little bit more.

She was still in his heart, as deeply and profoundly as she had been when they'd been seeing each other. He didn't want to love her anymore and knew that she certainly didn't love him, but he didn't know how to stop loving her. Over the past week it had become the thing that he did better than anything else.

He'd known when he'd gotten involved in this case that it was going to end badly. He could live with a broken heart, but if he didn't figure out how to save Hope, he knew he'd break Grace's heart once again. Charlie wasn't sure he could live with that.

As Grace stared out at the passing scenery, she was surprised to realize she was thinking of her mother. There were times when she glanced at herself in the mirror and saw a glimpse of the woman who had deserted them.

How could a woman who'd been a loving mother and good wife just pack her bags and leave without a backward glance?

And how long did it take before thoughts of her didn't hurt anymore?

She hadn't told anyone about Elizabeth, although she was sure most people in town knew about the vanishing act. Now she wanted to talk about it, especially to Charlie. She turned to look at him.

He looked so amazingly handsome, so cool and in control. She knew it was a façade, that he was worried about Hope, about her.

"You've asked me several times over the last couple of days about my mother." She tried to ignore the coil of tension that knotted tight in her stomach.

He shot her a quick glance. "You said she was out of the country."

She twisted her fingers together in her lap,

fighting both the anger and despair the conversation worked up inside her. "The truth is I don't have any idea where she is."

He said nothing, obviously waiting for her to explain.

She sighed and stared out the window for a long moment, then looked at him once again. "Two years ago while William was at a meeting and Hope was at school, my mother apparently packed a couple of suitcases and left."

Charlie frowned. "And you don't know where she went?"

"Don't have a clue." Grace tried to force a light tone but couldn't. She heard the weight of her pain hanging in her words. "I don't know where she went or why she left us without an explanation."

"And you haven't heard from her since?"

"Not a letter, not a postcard, nothing." She twisted her fingers more tightly together. "I don't mind so much for me. I mean, I'm a grown woman, but how could she walk out on Hope?"

"What did William have to say about it?" he asked.

"He said they'd had a fight the night before. At first he thought she'd just gone to a friend's house to cool off and would be back before nightfall. But she didn't come home that day, or the next, or the next. He was utterly heartbroken."

"Did you go to the sheriff?"

"Yeah, but a lot of good it did us. Jim Ramsey was the sheriff at the time. Did you know him?"

He nodded. "I know there was a big scandal about

his involvement in a murder and that Zack stepped into his shoes."

"William went to file a missing persons report, but Ramsey insisted there wasn't much he could do. Mom was of legal age. She'd taken her clothes and things with her, and if she didn't want to be a wife and mother anymore that was her right."

She'd had no right, Grace thought. She'd left behind three broken hearts that would never heal. "William hired a private investigator to search for her, but he never had anything to report, he never had a lead to follow."

Charlie was quiet for a long moment. "Why didn't you tell me this when we were seeing each other? It must have happened right before we met."

"Oh Charlie, there were a lot of important things we didn't talk about when we were together. We talked about whether we wanted to go out to dinner or stay in. You talked about your work and I talked about mine, but we didn't talk about what was going on with our lives when we were apart."

"You're right," he said flatly. "And it was one of the biggest mistakes we made. We should have talked about the important things."

Too late now. Grace looked out the window once again while a plethora of thoughts whirled through her head. It seemed as if the last two years of her life had been nothing more than a continuous journey of loss. First her mother, then Charlie, then William. And if something didn't break the case against her sister wide open, then Hope would be another loss.

A black, yawning despair rose up inside her. She'd been strong through it all, focused on getting from one day to the next without allowing herself any weakness.

At this moment, sitting next to the man who'd betrayed her trust, with thoughts of her mother and Hope heavy in her heart, she felt more alone than ever before.

"If I lose Hope, I won't have anything else to hang onto," she said. "My entire family has been ripped away from me, and I don't understand any of it."

"I'm going to see what I can do to find your mother," Charlie said.

She looked at him in surprise. "How are you going to do that?"

"I doubt if Jim Ramsey ever did anything to find her. It's tough for somebody to just disappear. She had a driver's license and tax records. With her Social Security number, we can start a search."

Grace frowned thoughtfully. "At this point, I'm not sure I care about finding her. Betrayal is a tough thing to get past."

He flashed her a quick glance. "Forgiveness is the first step on a path to healing."

"Forgiveness is for fools," she exclaimed with a touch of bitterness.

They didn't speak again for the remainder of the drive. The Beacon Juvenile Detention Center was on the south side of Oklahoma City. Set on twenty acres of hard, red clay, the building was a low, flat structure surrounded by high fences and security cameras.

The place had a cold, institutional look that Grace found horrifying.

As Charlie parked in the lot designated for visitors, a lump formed in Grace's throat as she thought of her sister inside.

Hope had never been anywhere but in the loving environment of William's home. How could she possibly cope with being locked up in this place with its barbed wire and truly bad kids?

"She doesn't belong here, Charlie," she said, as the two of them walked toward the entrance. "She isn't like the other kids in this place."

"I know, but right now there's nothing we can do about it." He reached for her hand, and again she was struck by how he seemed to know exactly what she needed and when.

She clung tightly to his hand, feeling as if it were an anchor to keep her from going adrift. The afternoon heat radiated up from the concrete walk, and Grace kept her gaze focused on the door.

Once inside, Charlie identified himself as Hope's lawyer and Grace as her sister. They were told to lock up their personal items, including Charlie's belt, and then were led to a small interview room with security cameras in all four corners and a guard in a khaki uniform outside the door.

Grace sat at the table with Charlie at her side and waited for her sister to be escorted inside. "We need to go back to the house, Charlie. We need to tear apart both William's and Hope's rooms to see if we can come up with something that will exonerate Hope."

"The sheriff and his men have already been through everything at the house," he said.

"Maybe they missed something." She heard the despair in her own voice. Being in this place made her feel desperate, for herself and for her sister. "You've got to do something, Charlie. I can't lose Hope."

"Grace, look at me." His eyes were dark, his gaze intense. "Right now we can't do anything to get Hope out of here. What I have to do is be prepared for when her trial comes up and make sure I do my job then. You told me when you came to me that it was because you needed a sneaky devil, and I was as close to the devil as you could find. You have to be patient now and trust that when the time is right, this sneaky devil will do his job."

Grace drew a tremulous sigh, the hysteria that had momentarily gripped her assuaged by the confidence she saw shining in Charlie's eyes.

At that moment the door opened and Hope walked in.

Charlie could tell the hour had passed too quickly for the two sisters, but at least Grace was leaving with the knowledge Hope was physically all right, although she was frightened and depressed.

It twisted his heart seeing the two of them together, how they'd clung to each other. Grace had remained calm and confident in front of Hope, assuring her that everything was going to be all right. It was only as they left the place that she seemed to wilt beneath the pressure and remained unusually silent.

They stopped on the way home for dinner at a little café that advertised itself as having the best barbecue in the state. The boast was vastly exaggerated. It was a quiet ride back, and Charlie could tell Grace's thoughts were on the sister she'd left behind. The sun was sinking low in the sky as they reached the edge of Cotter Creek.

He'd been stunned by what she'd told him about her mother. Charlie knew about grieving for a mother. He'd been devastated by the loss of his mother, and he'd had four years of preparing himself for her death. The death of a woman with cancer was understandable. The disappearance of a mother was not.

Hope was all she had left, and if he didn't manage to somehow come up with a defense for the young girl, then Grace would be truly alone and would probably hate him all over again.

He couldn't let that happen. As they drove down Main Street, he finally broke the silence that had grown to mammoth proportions. "We'll go back to the house tomorrow. I'm not sure we'll find anything helpful, but we'll search those rooms and see if anything turns up. I'll call Zack tomorrow and see if he's come up with anything new. We'll talk to Justin's roommate again and try to find a crack in the alibi."

He pulled up in her driveway and turned to look at her, wanting to take away the unusual slump of her shoulders and the dark look of defeat radiating from her eyes. He would prefer them filled with icy disdain.

"I swear to God, I'll make this right," he exclaimed. "I'll do everything in my power to make it right."

She broke eye contact with him and unfastened her seat belt. When she looked back at him, her eyes were filled with warmth, and she leaned across the seat and placed her lips on his.

Swift hunger came alive in him as he tasted those lips he'd dreamed about for so long. When she opened her mouth to him, he wanted to get her out of the car, take her into his arms and feel the press of her body against his, tangle his hands in her lush, silky hair.

The scent of her filled his head, dizzying him as the kiss continued. Charlie had always loved to kiss Grace. Her soft, full lips were made for kissing.

She broke the kiss long before he wanted her to and then opened her car door. "Don't bother walking me in," she said, as if to let him know the kiss had been the beginning and end of anything physical between them.

"Are you confusing me on purpose?" he asked, his voice thick and husky with the desire that still coursed hot and thick through his blood.

"I just figure if I'm confused you should be, too," she said, only adding to his bewilderment. "Call me in the morning to set up a time to go to the house." She slid out of the car and straightened up.

From the corner of his eye, Charlie saw a figure step around the side of her house. Everything seemed to happen in slow motion. He saw the figure raise an arm, heard the report of the gun and at the same time screamed Grace's name.

Chapter 8

Grace leapt back into the car just as she heard a metallic *ping* above her head.

"Stay down," Charlie cried, as he threw the car into reverse and burned rubber out of her driveway. She screamed and hunkered down in the seat as the passenger window exploded, sending glass showering over her back.

Her heart pounded so hard that she felt sick as Charlie steered the car like a guided missile. Her mind stuttered, trying to understand what just happened.

Somebody had shot at her. A bullet had narrowly missed her head. The words screamed through her head but didn't make sense.

As she started to sit up, Charlie pressed on the

back of her head to keep her contorted in the seat, and below the window level.

"Stay down. Are you all right? Did he hit you?" The urgency in his voice made every muscle in her body begin to tremble as the reality of what had just happened set in.

"No, I'm all right. I'm okay." Her voice was two octaves higher than normal, and she felt a hysterical burst of laughter welling up inside her. "If somebody is going to try to kill you, it's great when he's not a good shot."

Her laughter turned into a sob. "My God, somebody just tried to kill me, Charlie. What's going on with my life?"

"I don't know." His hand on the back of her head became a caress. "You can get up now. I don't think anyone is following us."

Tentatively she straightened to a sitting position, but she couldn't control the quivering of her body. "Did you see who he was?"

"No, he was in the shadows of the house and everything happened too damned fast. I'm taking you to my place tonight."

"If you think I'm going to argue with you, you're mistaken." She wrapped her arms around herself, attempting to warm the icy chill that possessed her insides.

"First we're going to take a couple of detours to make sure we're not being followed." As if to prove the point, he turned off Main, careened down a tree-lined street and then turned again onto another street.

"Charlie, why would somebody want to kill me?"

"I don't know, Grace. The first thing we're going to do when we get to my place is call Zack West. We need to report what happened."

He cursed beneath his breath. "I didn't see this coming. Jesus, if you hadn't jumped when you did, he would've nailed you."

Her trembling grew more intense. "Don't remind me." She brushed away the pieces of glass that clung to her. Her head pounded where she'd been hit before and she felt like she might throw up. "You're going to need a new window."

"That's the least of our problems right now," he replied, his voice still tense as his gaze continually darted to his rearview mirror.

They didn't speak again until they reached Charlie's ranch. He parked in front of the porch, got out of the car and came around to help her out.

It was only after she collapsed on his sofa that the shivering began to ease. As he got on the phone to call Zack, she stared out the window and replayed that moment when she'd seen the dark figure just out of the shadows, sensed imminent danger and dove back into the car.

What if she'd waited a second longer? What if he'd pulled the trigger a second sooner? The trembling she thought she had under control began again, and tears pressed hot in her eyes.

Somebody had tried to kill her. Why? *Why?* When Charlie hung up the phone, she looked at him, and he pulled her up into his arms.

"It's okay now. You're safe here," he said, as he held her tight. She burrowed her head into the crook of his neck, breathing in the familiar scent of him as her heartbeat crashed out of control with the residual fear.

He ran his hands up and down her back as he whispered in her ear words meant to soothe. Her trembling finally stopped, but still she remained in his embrace, unwilling to let go of him until the cold knot in her stomach had completely warmed.

There was a feeling of safety in Charlie's strong arms, and she needed that sense of security after what had just happened.

Finally she stepped back from him and sank to the sofa. "I can't believe this," she said, as Charlie began to pace back and forth in front of her. "How could this be happening to me?"

He went to the window and looked out, then began to pace once again, his lean body radiating with energy. "In light of what just happened, there's no way I think that the attack in the store was an attempted robbery," he said.

The cold chunk in her stomach re-formed as she stared at him in horror. "You think it was the same man as tonight? That he wanted to kill me that night in the store?"

"That would be a reasonable assumption. Give me a dollar."

"What?" She stared at him blankly as he held out his hand.

"Give me a dollar," he repeated.

She grabbed her purse from the sofa and pulled one out and handed it to him. "What's that for?"

He shoved the bill into his pocket. "You just hired me to be your professional bodyguard." His eyes were dark and simmered with a banked flame. "From now on you won't go anywhere, do anything, without me at your side. Until we know what's going on and who wants you dead, it isn't safe for you to be anywhere alone."

Grace leaned back against the sofa. Her life was spinning out of control and she didn't know why. Somebody wanted her dead, but she didn't know who. "Where's Rosa?" she asked, surprised that the housekeeper hadn't made an appearance yet.

"Today is her day off. She won't be back here until sometime tomorrow afternoon." Charlie once again moved to the window and peered outside, his back rigid with tension.

"Do you think whoever it was might come here?" she asked, fear leaping back into her voice. "If he recognized you, then what's to stop him from coming here and trying to get me again?"

Charlie turned away from the window and looked at her. "I won't let that happen." He walked over to the wooden desk in one corner of the room and opened the bottom drawer. "From now on anywhere we go there will be four of us. You and me and Smith and Wesson." He pulled out an automatic, checked the clip, then stuck the gun in his waistband at his back.

"I'm a hell of a shot and won't hesitate to pull the trigger if I think it's necessary," he added.

The sound of car tires crunching the gravel of the driveway drifted inside, and he turned back to the window. "It's Zack."

He opened the door to admit the lawman, and for the next twenty minutes Grace and Charlie explained to Zack what happened at her house and how it had been too dark for either of them to identify the man.

"You should be able to find a couple of slugs in my car," Charlie said. "One went into the passenger side and the other one shot out the window."

Zack nodded and looked at Grace. "And you don't have any idea who this person might be? No spurned boyfriends, no business problems of any kind?"

Grace shook her head. "I can't imagine who might want to hurt me. Do you think this has something to do with William's murder?"

Zack frowned. "I don't know what to think. I'll collect what evidence I can from Charlie's car and send some of my deputies over to your house to check for further evidence."

"There's something else I'd like for you to do," Charlie said. "Two years ago Grace's mother, Elizabeth, disappeared. I intend to do an Internet search to see if I can find out anything about where she might be right now, but you have better access to government records and can go places I can't. Would you check it out and see if you can find where she might be living now?"

"You think she might have something to do with all this?" Zack asked.

"No, that's impossible," Grace exclaimed. Her

mother might have deserted them, but she'd never have anything to do with the terrible things happening now.

Charlie and Zack exchanged a look that let Grace know they weren't as sure about her mother's innocence. "I'll check it all out and get back to you sometime tomorrow," Zack said. "I'm assuming that you'll be here?"

Grace nodded. "I don't want to go home right now."

Zack nodded with understanding. "That's a good idea. I recommend you don't go anywhere alone unless absolutely necessary and then take precautions for your own safety."

He got up from the chair where he'd been sitting, a weary frown on his face. "I don't know what in the hell is going on around here, but I'd sure like to get to the bottom of it."

"This has to put a new light on Hope's case," Grace said.

"We don't know that this incident is tied to William's murder," Zack replied. "And if it is, it doesn't necessarily do anything positive for Hope's case. The argument could be made that with you dead, Hope is the sole beneficiary of William's fortune."

Grace gasped. "That's a ridiculous argument," she exclaimed.

"I assume you'll be checking out Justin Walker's whereabouts for this evening," Charlie said.

"He's top on my list," Zack replied.

"You might also check out Hank Weatherford," Grace said. "Apparently there was some tension between him and William about some land William owns that butts up next to Hank's place."

Zack nodded. "Anything else you think of, no matter how small, call me."

"I'll walk you out," Charlie said, and the two men left the house.

Grace stared blankly at the front door, her mind reeling with everything that had happened—with all the possibilities of who might be responsible.

Did Hank want that five acres badly enough to kill for it? It seemed ridiculous to even consider such a thing, but thinking that Hope had somehow master-minded William's murder—and the attempted murder of Grace herself—in order to get all his money seemed equally ridiculous.

The other possibility—her mother—flirted at the edges of her mind, and although she wanted to dismiss it completely out of hand, she couldn't.

Pain blossomed in Grace's chest. Thoughts of Elizabeth always brought enormous grief, but this was different—more raw.

Maybe her mother had found another man and didn't know that William had changed his will so she was no longer the sole beneficiary. Perhaps she and her new man had decided to take out everyone who stood in the way of her getting that money.

It sounded crazy and sick, but Grace had seen enough to know that money could twist people into ugly semblances of themselves.

Or maybe what happened tonight had nothing to do with William's murder. *Somebody tried to kill me.* The words whirled around in her head, and again the cold knot retied itself in her chest.

She needed to think of something else, anything else. What she needed to do was make arrangements yet again for somebody else to open the store in the morning. She wasn't sure she'd be in at all.

Grace picked up Charlie's phone and dialed Dana's cell phone number. She answered on the second ring. "Dana, I hate to bother you, but could you open the store in the morning and work until Stacy comes in for her evening shift at four?"

"You know it's no problem," Dana replied. "I love working at the store. I'm just waiting for the time that you start sending me on buying trips, and I can take on more responsibility."

"What would that handsome husband of yours do without you if I sent you out of town?"

Dana laughed. "That handsome husband of mine would just have to cope, wouldn't he? Everything all right, Grace?"

"No, not really, but I appreciate your help with the store. I'll be in touch sometime tomorrow," she said, as Charlie came back through the door.

She hung up the phone. "That was Dana. I called her so she could open the store in the morning. She's a real jewel. Sometimes I don't know what I'd do without her." She was rambling, embracing thoughts of the store to keep away other, more troubling ideas.

"She wants to start going on buying trips for me. She has great taste. I probably should let her go."

Charlie's face blurred as tears filled her eyes. "She would do a good job."

"Grace," he said gently. "Why don't we get you settled in bed? Things won't look so grim in the morning." He held out his hand to her.

She took his hand and stood with a small laugh. "Somehow I don't think sunshine is going to fix any of this."

"Who knows? Maybe tomorrow Zack will find something that will identify your attacker."

She used her free hand to wipe at her tear-filled eyes. "I didn't know you were such an optimist, Charlie," she said, as they walked down the hallway toward the guest room she'd stayed in before.

"What are we going to do?" she asked when they reached the doorway. "How are you going to be my bodyguard, prepare a defense case for Hope and investigate all this? You aren't Superman."

He reached up and touched her cheek with a gentle smile. "Let me worry about it. You'd be surprised at what I'm capable of when I put my mind to it."

"Are you capable of getting me something to sleep in? I don't have anything."

He nodded. "How about one of my T-shirts?"

"Perfect," she agreed.

He dropped his hand from her face. "I'll be right back." He disappeared into the room at the far end of the hallway and returned a moment later with both a T-shirt and a toothbrush still in the package. "Try to get some sleep. We'll figure it all out in the morning," he said, handing her the items.

She nodded. "I'll see you in the morning." As he murmured a good-night, she closed the door between them and prayed that sleep would claim her quickly and banish all the horrible thoughts and images from her mind.

Rage, revenge or reward.

Charlie sat in his chair in the darkened living room and worked the motives for murder around in his head. No matter how he twisted everything, he couldn't make sense of it.

His heart accelerated in rhythm as he thought of that moment when he'd seen the figure in the shadows, watched as the figure raised his arm and knew that Grace was in danger. His heart had stopped then and hadn't resumed its regular, steady beat until they'd pulled up here at the ranch.

Moonlight filtered through the trees and into the window, making dancing patterns across the living room floor. He stared at the shifting patterns, as if in staring at them long enough something would make sense. Although he hadn't wanted to show his fear to Grace, the truth was he was afraid for her.

It was bad enough that somebody had tried twice to kill her, but almost as troubling was not having a clue as to the identity of her perpetrator.

Owning and operating a dress shop wasn't exactly a high-risk profession, and she'd insisted to Zack that there weren't any spurned lovers, no stalker boyfriends, nothing that could explain what was going on.

So what *was* going on? A dead man, a child facing

trial and two attempted murders. As crazy as it sounded, Charlie's thoughts kept returning to the missing mother. She was the one piece of the puzzle that remained a complete mystery.

Why had she left? Where was she now? After Grace went to bed, Charlie had done a cursory Internet search for her but found nothing.

The fact that Grace hadn't told him about her mother when they'd been dating indicated to him how little she'd thought of their relationship. He hadn't been important enough in her life to share that particular heartbreak.

He reached up and touched his bottom lip, where the feel of that brief kiss in the car lingered. Why had she kissed him? And if their relationship had meant nothing to her, then why did she hate him for how it had ended?

To say that she confused him was an understatement. What he didn't find confusing at all were his feelings for her. He loved her. It was as simple and as complicated as that. He'd never stopped loving her.

And she would never forgive him.

He released a weary sigh and glanced at the clock with the luminous dial on the desk. After two. Time to go to bed. He wasn't accomplishing anything here and needed to be fresh and alert tomorrow.

When he stood to go to his bedroom, he saw her standing in the doorway. By the light of the moon he could see her clearly—her tousled hair, the sleek length of her legs beneath the T-shirt, which fell to midthigh, and the fear that widened her eyes.

"Bad dream?" he asked, trying to ignore the white-hot fire of desire in the pit of his stomach.

"I don't need to be asleep to have bad dreams," she replied, her voice filled with stress. "I haven't been able to sleep. I've just been tossing and turning. I can't get it all out of my head—the noise of the bullet hitting the car, knowing that if I hadn't jumped into the car when I did another bullet might have hit me."

"You want something to eat? Maybe a glass of milk?" Although he tried to keep his gaze focused on her face, it slid down just low enough to see her breasts—her nipples hard against the cotton material. He quickly glanced up once again as every muscle in his body tensed. "Maybe putting something in your stomach will help."

"No, thanks. I'm not hungry." She took a step toward him, and he saw the tremble of her lower lip. "I was wondering if maybe I could sleep with you."

He knew she didn't mean sleep as a euphemism for anything else. She was afraid to be alone, and even though he knew how hard—no, how torturous it was going to be to lie next to her and not touch her, he nodded his head. "Sure, if that's what you want. My bed is big enough for the two of us."

"Thank you," she said gratefully.

He followed her down the hallway to the master bedroom and wondered how in the hell he was going to survive the night.

Chapter 9

Charlie tried to halt the rapid beating of his heart as she stood next to the bed. After he pulled down the covers, she slid in and curled up on her side facing him.

He placed his gun on the nightstand, then self-consciously unbuttoned his shirt and shrugged it off. It was silly to feel shy about undressing in front of her. She'd seen him naked more times than he could count, but that was before, in a different time under different circumstances.

Kicking off his shoes, he glanced at her to see that her eyes were closed. That made it easier for him to get out of his jeans. Normally he slept naked, but tonight he got beneath the sheet wearing his briefs, feeling as if he needed a barrier between them, even if it was just thin cotton.

"'Night, Charlie," she said softly, as he turned off the bedside lamp.

"Sleep tight, Grace," he replied. He squeezed his eyes closed, willing sleep to come fast, but how could he sleep with the scent of her eddying in the air and her body heat radiating outward to him?

He tried to count sheep, but each one of them had silky blond hair and a killer body beneath a white T-shirt. He knew she wasn't sleeping, either. He could tell by her uneven breathing that she was still awake.

They remained side by side, not touching in any way for several agonizingly long minutes. He gasped in surprise as she reached out and laid a warm hand on his chest.

"Grace," he said, her name nothing more than a strangled sigh that hissed out of him.

She scooted closer to him and trailed her fingers across the width of his upper body, tangling them in his tuft of chest hair. "What?" she whispered.

"You can't lie here next to me and touch me like that and not know that you're starting something."

"Maybe I want to start something." The words were a hot whisper against his neck. "I want you to hold me, Charlie. I want you to make love to me and take away the coldness inside me."

There was nothing he wanted more, but he didn't move. "You've had a scare, Grace. It's only natural that you'd reach out to somebody, but I don't want you to do something tonight that you'll regret in the morning."

Once again her hand swept across his chest and

he held his breath. "As long as you understand that it isn't the beginning of anything, that it's just sex, then I won't regret anything in the morning," she replied.

Jeez, how many men would have loved to hear from a woman that it was just about sex and nothing else? Still he hesitated. He didn't want to give her another reason to hate him. He told himself that one of them had to be strong.

She moved closer, molding herself against his side. "I know you still want me, Charlie. I've seen it in your eyes; I've felt it in your touch. I want you now. Not forever, but just for now."

Even though he would have preferred now and forever, he wasn't strong enough to stop himself from turning to her. Their lips met in an intense kiss that tasted of the sweet familiarity of past liaisons and of present fires.

Just that easily he was lost in her, in the taste of her, the scent of her and the heat of her body, so close to his. He cupped her face in his hands as the kiss continued, their tongues swirling together as their breaths quickened.

He pulled her into his arms, half across his body as his hands caressed her back and made their way to the bottom of the T-shirt.

He broke the kiss and plucked at the shirt. "Take it off. I want to feel your body next to mine."

She sat up and in one smooth movement pulled the shirt up and over her head. She tossed it to the floor at the end of the bed, then went into his arms once again.

Her soft, supple skin was hot against his, and he cupped her breasts, his thumbs moving over her hard nipples. The tiny gasp she emitted only served to ratchet up his desire.

He wanted her moaning like she once had beneath him, making those mewling noises that had always driven him wild.

She rolled over on her back, and he took one of her nipples into his mouth as she tangled her fingers in his hair. He teased first one, then the other nipple, sucking then flicking his tongue to give her the most pleasure.

"Charlie," she moaned, his name a sweet plea on her lips.

His hand moved down her flat stomach and lingered at the waist of her panties. Touching her was sheer pleasure, the smoothness of her skin making his blood thicken as he grew hard.

"Take them off," she said, and lifted her buttocks from the bed so he could pull the panties down and off. With her naked, he quickly took off his briefs. Then they came together—hot flesh and hotter kisses.

Although he was hungry for her, he wanted to take his time. He wanted it slow. He wanted to pretend that they had never stopped being lovers, that there was nothing bad between them.

He re-memorized the sweet curves of her hips, the silky length of her legs. His lips found all the places he knew would stoke her pleasure higher, and the taste of her drove him half mindless.

Grace had always been an active participant in lovemaking, and this time was no different. Her mouth and hands seemed to be everywhere—behind his ear, on his chest above his crashing heartbeat, along his inner thigh.

Knowing that if he allowed her to continue with her caresses, it was going to be over before it began, Charlie pushed her onto her back once again, and his fingers found her damp heat.

She arched her hips to meet his touch as she whimpered his name. Every muscle in her body tensed, and he knew she was almost there, almost over the edge. He quickened his touch and felt the moment when her climax crashed down on her. She froze and then seemed to melt as she cried his name over and over again.

Knowing he was about to lose control, he quickly disengaged from her and fumbled in his nightstand for a condom. His hands trembled uncontrollably as he pulled on the protection and then eased into her with a hiss of pleasure.

He froze, afraid that the slightest movement would end it all. The moonlight filtered through the curtains, dappling her face with enough light that he could see the bright shine of her eyes, a pulse beating madly in the side of her neck.

She closed her eyes, and he felt her tighten her muscles around him, creating exquisite pleasure for him. Her fingers dug into his lower back, and he slowly eased his hips back, then stroked deep into her.

The rush of feelings that filled him was overwhelming, not just the physical ones, but the emotional ones as well. She was hot, sexy and felt like home. She scared him more than any potential killer they might face.

He had confidence that he could keep her safe and sound from any threat, but he didn't know how to make her forgive him. He wanted her to be his woman forever, but she'd made it clear she was his just for now.

He'd had his chance with her and blown it. Now his job was to fix her life so that she could once again move on without him.

Grace woke up with the light of dawn drifting through the window and Charlie spooned around her back. She remained still, relishing the feeling of safety his arms provided, the warmth of his body against her.

Making love with him had been as magical last night as it had been eighteen months ago when they'd been an item. Charlie was a passionate man, a thoughtful lover who never took his own pleasure before giving pleasure to her. Her body still glowed warm with the residual aftermath of the night of love.

Had last night been a mistake? Definitely.

If she allowed herself, she could be as in love with Charlie as she had been before, but she wouldn't allow it. There was still a simmering rage inside her where he was concerned, a place where forgiveness could find no purchase.

She slid out of bed, wanting to get up before he awakened. She knew how much Charlie loved morning sex, and although there was a part of her that would have welcomed another bout of lovemaking with him, she didn't want to be available for compounding her mistake.

The last thing she needed to do was think about Charlie and her confusing feelings for him. What she needed to do was figure out why somebody would want her dead.

She used the shower in the guest room, hoping to let Charlie rest for as long as he could. She'd fallen asleep before him the night before and had no idea when he'd finally drifted off.

Charlie was mistaken. Nothing seemed clearer in the light of day, she thought, as she stood beneath a hot stream of water. William was still dead. Somebody was gunning for her and Hope was facing life in prison. No amount of morning sun could put a happy spin on things.

When she was dressed, she went into the kitchen, surprised to find Charlie making coffee. Apparently he'd been in the shower at the same time as her. His hair was damp, and he smelled of minty soap and that cologne that had always driven her half wild.

"Good morning," he said, and gave her a tentative glance.

"Don't worry, there aren't going to be any repercussions from last night," she assured him, as she sat at the table.

"That's good. I was worried that you'd accuse me

of taking advantage of you," he replied, pouring them each a cup of the fresh brew.

"I think I was definitely the one taking advantage last night," she replied dryly.

He set the mugs on the table then took the seat across from her. "Grace, we need to talk. We need to talk about us."

She held up a hand and shook her head. "Please, Charlie, don't." She steeled her heart against him, against the flash of vulnerability she saw in his eyes. "There's so much going on in my life right now. I can't think about anything else except getting Hope out of that horrible place and trying to figure out why somebody tried to shoot me last night."

He held her gaze for a long minute and then nodded reluctantly. "Okay, we won't do it now," he agreed, but there was a subtle warning in his words that let her know this wasn't finished—*they* weren't finished.

But they were, she thought, and the old, familiar anger rose up inside her. His betrayal hurt just like her mother's had, and she'd never forgive her mother nor was she ever likely to forgive him. She'd be a fool to trust him with her heart again, and Grace wasn't anybody's fool.

"You need to decide if you want to stay here with me or if you want me to stay at your place with you," he said. "There's no way I want you staying anywhere all alone right now."

She wanted to protest the plan, but she knew she couldn't return to her life as if nothing had happened. She frowned thoughtfully. "I'd really prefer to stay at my own place, but don't you need to be here at the ranch?"

"I've got a good foreman who can see to things," he replied.

Wrapping her fingers around her mug, she frowned again. "I hate the idea of taking you away from your life here."

He smiled, the gesture warming the gray of his eyes. "You bought my services as a bodyguard for a dollar. Until this thing is resolved, wherever you go, I go. If you want to stay at your place, then all I need to do is pack a bag."

"If you don't mind, I'd appreciate it," she said. Maybe her world would feel more normal if she were home among her familiar things. "I'd like to go back to the house today." She took a sip of her coffee and then continued. "We should talk to Lana and Leroy again. Maybe they will have remembered something helpful."

"I think they would have called if that was the case," he said. "But, if you want to touch base with them, we can do that. Have you thought about what you intend to do with the house and the property?"

"No. I suppose eventually I'll sell. I'll never live in the house, and I don't want it sitting empty forever." Grief for William pierced through her. He'd loved that house so much.

"The real estate market isn't great right now, but I imagine a home like that will move fairly quickly."

"I need to give Lana and Leroy a heads-up that at

some point they'll need to find another place to live. At least with the money William left to Lana I know they won't be out on the street." She sipped her coffee, thinking about everything that needed to be done to settle William's estate.

Somebody tried to kill you yesterday. The words jumped unbidden into her head. She took another sip of her coffee and tried to think of a single person she'd upset or offended.

"This can't be personal," she said aloud.

"What?" Charlie looked at her in confusion.

"Whoever is trying to kill me. It has to be about something other than dislike or anger at me personally. I know it sounds conceited, but I can't think of anyone who could hate me. I run a dress shop, for God's sake. I've never had a problem with anyone in town."

"We have a missing mother, a dead stepfather, a sister who we believe has been set up to spend the rest of her life in prison, and somebody trying to kill you. It's like somebody is trying to erase the entire Covington family."

"Surely you don't think my mother's disappearance has anything to do with what's happening now," she said.

He sipped his coffee, a new frown creasing his forehead. "I don't know. Last night I did a quick search on the computer for your mother but got no results." He swept a hand through his thick, dark hair. "I keep working everything around in my head trying to make sense of it, but I can't get a handle on it. Do you have a will?"

"No, I haven't gotten around to making one yet."

"So, if something happened to you, everything you own would go to Hope as your sole living relative?"

"I guess." She narrowed her eyes. "Charlie, I don't care how bad this looks, Hope wouldn't do this. Please, don't lose faith in her innocence."

"I'm just looking at all the angles," he said, and took another drink of his coffee. "Why don't we eat some breakfast and head to your place? I'll stow my stuff there, and then we can head over to the mansion to see what we can find."

It was after nine when they left the ranch to go to Grace's house. Charlie had a small suitcase in the backseat and his automatic pistol in a holster beneath his jacket.

The knowledge that he was carrying a gun to protect her sent a new rivulet of disquiet through her. The shooting the night before and the attack at the store had had a dreamlike quality to them, but his gun made them terrifyingly real.

"I really appreciate you staying at my place," she said, as they drove down Main Street toward her street. "I have a nice guest room where I hope you'll be comfortable." She wanted to make it clear there would be no repeat of last night, that she had no intention of him sleeping next to her in her bed.

"I'm sure I'll be fine," he replied. "You need to stop by the store for anything?"

"No. Dana will have things well under control. She should have a shop of her own. She has all the skills to run her own business."

"You've certainly made a success of it," he observed.

She frowned. "I suppose." Yes, she had made a success of her shop, but at what price? Certainly in the last two years she'd kept too busy to nurture her relationship with her sister. A hollow wind blew through her as she thought of the choices she'd made.

She had plenty of friendly customers, but few friends, and when she'd needed somebody to hold her close, to take away her fear, there had been nobody except the man she'd once dated, a man who had broken her heart. Yeah, right, some success she'd made of her life.

The wind coming in from the broken window felt good on her face. Charlie had cleaned up the glass before they'd gotten into the car. The plan was for him to hire someone to come out to Grace's house to replace the window. They'd use her car for the remainder of the day.

When they reached her place, Charlie pulled up in the driveway and cut the engine. "I'll come around for you," he said, pulling his gun from his holster. "We'll walk together to the front door with you just in front of me. I don't want a repeat of last night."

As he got out of the car, the reality of the situation slammed into her. Somebody had tried to kill her last night. Somebody had tried to put a bullet in her head.

She gazed around her yard and the house, looking for a shadow, a movement that would indicate somebody lying in wait for them. A new knot of tension twisted in the pit of her stomach.

He opened her door and pulled her out and against his chest. They walked awkwardly toward her front door, with him acting as a human shield against danger.

Grace didn't realize she'd been holding her breath until she unlocked the door and stepped into the entry hall. It was only then that she breathed again.

"Stay right here and don't move," Charlie said. "I want to check out the house." He kept the front door open. "If somebody is in here, I'll let you know and want you to run to the car and drive to the sheriff's office." He handed her the car keys, then disappeared into the living room.

Grace's heart beat frantically with fight-or-flight adrenaline as she held the keys firmly in hand and waited for him to return. What if somebody was here—lying in wait for them? What if that somebody bashed Charlie over the head or shot him?

Once again her breath caught in her chest as she stood rigid with taut muscles—waiting...hoping that there was nobody inside.

Finally he came back, his gun back where it belonged. "It's okay," he said. A devilish gleam lit his eyes. "The purple bedroom is hot."

She laughed as the edge of tension faded. "The purple bedroom is mine. You get the one across from it. Why don't you put your things in there? I'm going to change my clothes before we leave again."

"I'll just go get my suitcase from the car," he said. As he went out the front door, Grace walked down the hallway to her bedroom.

She'd always loved the color purple in all its

glorious shades. When she'd moved into the house, she'd decided to indulge herself by painting the walls of her bedroom lilac and finding a royal purple satin spread for the bed. The end result gave the aura of both relaxation and hedonistic pleasure.

Her dresser top held framed photos along with an array of perfume bottles and lotion. She walked over to the dresser and looked at the pictures. There was one of Hope in a pair of footed Christmas pajamas, her face lit with a beautiful smile.

There was also one of William, Hope and Grace. It had been taken six months after her mother's disappearance. The three of them had been at a carnival, and although they all sported smiles on their faces, the smiles didn't quite reach their eyes.

She turned away from the bureau and unbuttoned her blouse, then walked to her closet. Maybe today they'd find something at the house that would exonerate Hope. Even though logically she knew that Zack and his men would have gone over the crime scene with a fine-tooth comb, she still clung to the belief that somehow she and Charlie would find something that the authorities had missed.

She leaned against the doorjamb for a long moment, staring at the clothes inside the closet. Grace was exhausted even though she'd slept soundly after making love with Charlie. It wasn't physical fatigue but rather a mental one.

She grabbed a short-sleeved blue blouse from a hanger, then turned around. A scream welled up inside her and exploded out as she saw a face at her window.

Chapter 10

The scream ripped through Charlie, electrifying him with terror. He pulled his gun and raced across the hallway into her room.

She stood in front of the closet, her face a pasty shade of white. "He was looking in my window," she managed to gasp.

That's all Charlie needed to hear. He tore out of her bedroom, down the hallway and out the front door. He raced around the side of her house and spied a tall, lean figure running toward the fence that surrounded her yard. It was a privacy fence, and there was no way in hell he'd be able to jump it.

"Stop, or I swear I'll shoot," Charlie yelled, as the man leapt up to grab the top of the fence.

Unsuccessful, the man fell back to the ground then turned to face Charlie. It was Justin Walker. His eyes widened to saucer size as he saw the gun Charlie held in his hand.

Instantly he raised his hands. "Hey man, don't shoot me."

"What are you doing here?" Charlie asked, his gun not wavering from the young man's midsection. "Did you come back here today to finish what you tried to do last night?"

Justin frowned. "Last night? Dude, I don't know what you're talking about."

He looked genuinely perplexed, but Charlie wasn't taking anything for granted. "Get inside the house. I'm calling the sheriff." He gestured with his gun for Justin to move.

"Hey man, there's no need to call the fuzz. I wasn't doing anything. I just wanted to talk to Grace, that's all. I wanted to talk to her alone." As he protested his innocence, he moved toward the house where Grace stood at the back door, her eyes wide with fear.

"You have any weapons?" Charlie asked, as they reached the back porch.

"Hell no. I didn't come here looking for trouble," he exclaimed.

"Well, you found it," Charlie said. Despite Justin's protests, Charlie quickly patted him down, making sure the young man had no weapons on him.

Grace opened the backdoor. "Justin, what are you doing here?" she asked. She seemed to relax as she realized Charlie had things under control.

When they got into the kitchen, Charlie gestured for Justin to sit at the table. "I just wanted to talk to you," Justin said to Grace. "I was just going to stand at the window and try to get your attention, but then you saw me and screamed, and I freaked and ran."

"Maybe we should just call Zack and let Justin explain everything to him," Charlie said.

"No, please, don't do that." Justin slumped in the chair, an air of defeat in his posture. "He already thinks I killed Hope's stepdad. I don't need any more trouble from him."

"What do you want to talk to me about?" Grace asked. She remained standing next to the counter on the other side of the room from Justin. Charlie was standing as well, his gun still clutched in his hand.

Justin swept a hand through his dark, unruly hair. "I wanted to ask you about Hope. I just wanted to know if she was okay."

"Why do you care? According to you, the two of you were just casual friends, hang-out buddies and nothing more," Grace replied.

Justin's cheeks colored with a tinge of pink. "She was nice to me, okay? I liked her. When she turned sixteen, we were going to start officially dating. I just wanted to know if she was doing all right, that's all."

"She's fine, coping as well as can be expected," Grace said.

"Where were you last night?" Charlie asked.

"I was home, with my roommate."

Charlie narrowed his eyes. "Your roommate is a pretty handy alibi whenever you need one."

This time the flush of color in Justin's cheeks was due to anger, not embarrassment. "I can't help it if it's the truth."

"Should we call Zack?" Charlie asked.

Grace studied Justin's face for a long moment and then shook her head. "No, just let him go. I think he's telling the truth."

"I am," Justin exclaimed.

Charlie wasn't so sure, but he complied with Grace's wishes. "Go on. Get out of here. But if I see you around Grace again, I won't wait for the sheriff to ask you questions. I'll beat your ass myself."

Justin didn't speak again. As Charlie lowered his gun, he jumped out of the kitchen chair and ran for the front door. Charlie followed, making sure he left the house.

When he returned to the kitchen, Grace still leaned against the cabinets. "You okay?" he asked.

She nodded. "Now we know there was definitely something romantic going on between Hope and Justin." She looked dispirited, as if she knew this new information would only make things worse for Hope. "It will be easy for the prosecution to make a case that Hope killed William because William wouldn't let her see Justin."

"It doesn't change anything," Charlie replied with a forced lightness. "Go change your clothes so we can get out of here."

As she left the room, Charlie tried to get the sound

of her scream out of his head. His heart had stopped when he'd heard her. He hoped he never heard that particular sound from her again.

A few minutes later they were in her car and headed to the Covington mansion. "I think tomorrow I just might stay in bed all day," she said with a sigh. "At least there won't be any surprises there."

"Unless I'm there with you," Charlie said, and wiggled his eyebrows up and down in Groucho Marx fashion. He wanted to make her laugh to ease the tension that thinned her lips and darkened her eyes.

He was rewarded as a small giggle escaped her. "You're wicked, Charlie Black," she exclaimed before sobering back up. "I hope you're as good a lawyer as you were two years ago. Hope is going to need every one of your skills."

"I've already requested that Zack give me copies of all the interviews he conducted with people immediately after the murder. I plan on getting all the discovery available to start building our case. Believe it or not, Grace, I'm working on it." He tapped the side of his head. "I do my best work in my head long before I commit anything to paper. I have a theory about murder."

"And what's that?"

"I call it the three *R*s. Most murders are committed for one of three reasons: rage, revenge or reward."

"And which category do you think William's murder falls into?" she asked.

He turned down off the main road and into the long Covington driveway. "I'm still trying to figure it out. The prosecuting attorney is probably going to argue rage—Hope's rage at a figure of authority who kept her from seeing the boy that she loved. Or he could possibly argue reward—that with William out of the picture she would be a very wealthy young lady."

She sighed. "Sounds grim."

He flashed her a reassuring grin. "Grim doesn't scare me. It just gets my juices flowing." He pulled up in front of the house and cut the engine, aware of Grace's gaze lingering on him. He unbuckled his seat belt and turned to look at her. "What?"

"Do you miss it? Being a lawyer? The adrenaline rush of the courtroom and the high stakes?"

He hesitated before answering, not wanting to give her a flippant response. "I'll tell you what I miss. I miss my father, who would have been proud of the man I've become over the last year. I regret the fact that I'm thirty-five years old and haven't gotten married and started a family of my own. To answer your question, no, there's absolutely nothing I miss about my old life." *Except you.*

The last two words jumped into his mind and for some reason irritated him. He wasn't sure if the target of his irritation was himself or Grace.

"Come on, let's get inside and see what we can find," he exclaimed.

Even though he had checked the rearview mirror constantly to make certain they hadn't been followed, he once again escorted her inside with his gun pulled and his body shielding hers.

Once they got inside, Charlie followed Grace to William's office, which was located in one of the bedrooms upstairs. As she sat at the desk and began to go through the drawers, he walked over to the window and stared out to the backyard. Grace still refused to go into the bedroom where William had been murdered, but Charlie had gone in and had found nothing to help find his killer.

He had little hope that she would find anything useful. She'd already been through the desk once before, but he knew she needed to do something to feel as if she were actively helping her sister.

Leroy had apparently been working hard. The flower beds in the backyard exploded in vivid blooms, with nary a weed in sight. The bushes were neatly trimmed and the grass was a lush green carpet.

Rage. Revenge. Reward. Somebody out there had a motive for killing William. If Justin and Hope had worked in concert to commit the murder, then why had she been passed out on the bed in an incriminating manner? Why didn't they just alibi each other?

Was it possible that the issue of those five acres had created such contention that Hank lost control and killed William? Hank was no young man, but it didn't take a lot of strength to stab a sleeping man in the back.

Charlie could smell Grace. Her dizzying scent not only fired his hormones, but also somehow touched his heart. Anger was building in him where she was concerned, an anger he didn't want to feel and certainly didn't want to acknowledge.

He knew he'd hurt her badly in the past, but he

was irritated by the fact that she refused to talk about it and clung to her sense of betrayal like it was a weapon to use against him at her whim.

He realized, though, that she was fragile now, and the last thing he wanted to do was add to the burdens she was already shouldering. He had to keep his emotions in check.

Once she had searched through the desk, she returned to Hope's bedroom. He stood at the door as she pulled open drawers and picked through the mess on the floor. She'd been through it all before and found nothing. He sensed her desperation but didn't know what to do to ease it.

It was almost three o'clock when he finally called a halt to her search. "Grace, there's nothing here," he said. "If there had been something, Zack would have found it, and if he missed anything, you would have found it by now."

She sat in the middle of Hope's bedroom floor, sorting through a box of keepsake items that belonged to her younger sister.

She put the lid back on the box and sighed. "I know you're right. I just feel compelled to do something to help. It doesn't feel right for me to work at the shop and go about my usual routine while everything else is falling apart."

"I know, but a daily routine is necessary, especially the part where we eat to stay strong. My stomach has been growling for the past hour."

She rose to her feet. "Why didn't you say something?"

He smiled and fought an impulse to reach out and tuck a stray strand of hair behind her ear. "I just did. But before we leave I'd like to check out the property that Hank and William had been arguing about."

She frowned at him. "Okay, but there really isn't anything there but a bunch of weeds and trees." Grace stood up, and they went downstairs.

"You once mentioned something about an old shed," he said, when they reached the front door. "You know what's in it?"

"Probably nothing. I think at one time it used to be a gardener's shed, but it hasn't been used in years." As she locked the door, Charlie once again gripped his gun.

He looked around the immediate area, seeking any threat that might come at them, at her. She turned from the door and stood just behind him.

The Covington place was isolated enough that it would be difficult for anyone to approach without being noticed. He felt no danger, saw nothing that would give him pause. While inside he'd spent much of the time at the windows, watching the road for any cars that didn't belong and checking the grounds for anything unusual.

"Where's that property?" he asked.

"Around back, behind Leroy and Lana's place."

"I want you to walk right in front of me. I don't think there's anyone around, but I don't want to take any chances."

"I'd like to stop by Lana's and let them know that I've decided to sell this place. The new owner might want to continue their services and let them remain in the cottage, but it's also possible they need to start making other plans."

The walk to the cottage was awkward, with her walking nearly on the top of his feet. As always, her nearness raised the simmering heat inside him, and he tried to ignore it as he kept focused on their surroundings.

Lana and Leroy weren't home. Nobody answered Grace's knock and no vehicles were parked in front of the place. "Maybe they both went to pick up Lincoln from school," Grace said.

"He seems like a nice kid." They headed for the side of the cottage.

"He's certainly the apple of their eyes," she replied. "Lana was pregnant when she married Leroy, and William and I were just grateful that he stepped up and did the right thing. It seems to have worked out well."

She pointed in the distance where the manicured lawn ended and an area of trees and overgrown brush began. "That's the land Hank was talking about. It never bothered William because it's so far away from the main house, but Hank's place is just on the other side, and I can understand why he'd want to see it cleaned up. The shed is on the other side of that big oak tree."

They headed toward the area where the shed was located. Charlie didn't want to leave any stone unturned.

He figured it was probably empty or full of gardening tools that had rusted and rotted over the years.

When they reached the wooden structure, Charlie returned his gun to his holster and eyed the old padlock on the door.

"I can't imagine why it would be locked," Grace said. "Nobody has used it in years. I wouldn't have any clue where to begin to look for the key."

"Who needs a key?" Charlie replied. He eyed the rotten wood around the lock on the door. Tensing his muscles, he slammed his shoulder into the door and was rewarded by splintering wood.

Another three hits and the door came away from the lock, allowing him to open it.

He pulled the door open just a bit and peered inside. The first thing he noticed was the unpleasant musty odor that wafted in the air. Then he saw the two flowered suitcases that sat on the floor just inside the door.

His heart began to bang against his ribs. Then he saw the sandal—a bright red woman's sandal. Inside it was the remains of a foot.

He reeled back and slammed the door. "We need to call Zack," he said, and turned to face Grace. Dread mingled with horror as he stared at her.

"Why? What's in there?" She tried to get past him to the door, but he stood his ground.

He grabbed her by the shoulders, his heart breaking for what he had to tell her. "Grace, stop. Listen to me."

She looked at him wildly, as if she knew what he was about to say. "Tell me, Charlie. What's inside the shed?"

"I'm sorry. I'm so damned sorry." He pulled her into his arms and held her tight, knowing she was going to need his strength. "Grace, I think it's your mother. Your mother's body is in the shed."

Chapter 11

Grace sat on the sofa in William's opulent living room, numb and yet as cold as the worst Oklahoma ice storm. She had yet to cry, although she knew eventually the numbness would pass and the pain would crash in.

It was late. Darkness had fallen, and still Zack and his men were processing the scene. Charlie was out there with them, but he'd insisted Zack leave a deputy with Grace.

Ben Taylor stood at the window, staring out in the distance where a faint glow of lights shone from the area behind the cottage.

For two years Grace had hated her mother for abandoning them. For two years she had cursed the name of the woman who had given birth to her. The anger was what had sustained her. Now it was gone and she had nothing left to hang on to.

She hadn't left them.

She'd been murdered.

The words flittered through Grace's head, but she couldn't grasp the concept, didn't yet feel the reality deep inside her.

The front door opened and a moment later Zack and Charlie walked into the room. Charlie immediately came to her side and sat next to her, his hand reaching for hers.

She allowed him to hold her hand. Somewhere in the back of her mind Grace realized his skin was warm against her icy flesh, but the warmth couldn't pierce through the icy shell that encased her.

"Zack wants to ask you a few questions," Charlie said gently.

"Of course." She looked at Zack, who sat in the chair across from them, his green eyes expressing a wealth of sympathy.

"Do you know of anyone your mother was having problems with at the time of her disappearance?" Zack asked.

"No." Her voice seemed to float from very far away.

Zack frowned. "Charlie mentioned that William had told you he and your mother had a fight the night before she disappeared."

She was having trouble concentrating. She felt as if she were in some sort of strange bubble, where things were happening around her and people were talking to her, but she really wasn't involved in any of it.

"Grace?" Charlie squeezed her hand.

She looked first at Charlie, then at Zack. "Yes, William told me they had an argument, but it wasn't a big deal. They were happily married, but like all couples they occasionally had disagreements."

She stared at Zack and then turned once again to gaze at Charlie. "What's happened to my family? Everyone has disappeared and now somebody is trying to make me disappear." Her voice had a strange, singsong quality.

"I need to get her home," Charlie said to Zack. "She's in shock."

"Yes, please take me home. I need to go to bed. I need to sleep. Things will be better in the morning, won't they, Charlie?"

He didn't answer her, but he wrapped an arm around her and pulled her against his side. "Zack, if you have any more questions for her, they can be asked tomorrow."

Zack nodded and stood at the same time Charlie helped her up from the sofa. At that moment Lana came flying into the room.

She looked around. "Is it true? Elizabeth is dead?" Zack nodded, and she began to sob.

Grace broke away from Charlie and went to her. She wrapped her arms around Lana and vaguely wondered why the housekeeper was crying for her mother and she wasn't.

"I need to ask you some questions," Zack said to Lana. "Both you and your husband."

Lana nodded and Grace stepped back from her.

"Do you know who would do this? Do you know who would kill my mother and pack her suitcases and stuff her in an old shed?"

"I don't know." Lana looked around wildly. "I don't understand any of this. First William and now your mother." Lana began to weep once again as Zack led her to a chair.

Charlie grabbed Grace by the arm. "Come on, let's get you home."

Once they were in the car, Grace leaned her head back and closed her eyes. "I'm so tired."

"We'll get you home and tucked into bed," he said.

"And I'm cold. I'm so cold. I don't feel like I'll ever be warm again." She wrapped her arms around herself and fought against the shivers that tried to take control.

"You will," he replied. "Eventually you'll get warm again and you'll laugh and enjoy life. Time, Grace. Give yourself time. It's true what they say about time healing all wounds."

Once again she closed her eyes. She knew eventually the agonizing grief over losing her mother would probably ease, but how could she get over her guilt? For two years she'd hated a woman who hadn't left them but instead had been brutally murdered.

Emotion swelled in her chest and made the very act of breathing difficult. She fought against it, afraid to let it take her—afraid that once she let it loose she would lose what little control she had left.

"Somebody must have hated us," she murmured, more to herself than to Charlie. "Somebody must hate us all, but I don't know who it could be."

She sighed in relief as Charlie pulled up in her driveway. All she wanted was to sleep—hopefully without dreams. It was the easiest way to escape the confusion and pain that had become her life.

Charlie helped her out of the car, and once they were inside he led her directly to her bedroom. She sat on the edge of the bed and tried to unbutton her blouse, but her fingers were all thumbs.

"Here, let me help," Charlie said. He crouched down in front of her and unfastened the buttons. There was nothing sexual in his touch, only a gentleness she welcomed as he pulled the blouse from her arms.

He retrieved her nightgown from the hook on the back of her bedroom door and carried it to her. "Here, while you put this on, I'll turn down the bed."

Dutifully she stood and took off her bra and pulled the nightgown over her head. Then she took off her pants, and by that time the bed was ready for her to crawl into.

She got beneath the covers and shivered uncontrollably. "Charlie, could you just hold me until I get warm?"

He quickly stripped down to his briefs and then slid beneath the sheets and pulled her into his arms. She welcomed the warmth of his skin as she shivered in his arms.

He stroked her hair and kissed her temple. "It's going to be all right," he said softly. "You're strong, Grace. You're one of the strongest women I've ever known. You're going to get through this."

"You don't understand. She wasn't just my

mother, she was my best friend." The words pierced through a layer of the protective bubble she'd been in since learning of her mother's death. "And I don't feel very strong right now." Tears burned her eyes as grief ripped through her.

Charlie seemed to sense the coming storm and tightened his arms around her. "Let it go, Grace," he said softly. "Just let it go."

"I never understood how she could have just walked away from me…from us. Oh God, Charlie, for two years I've hated a dead woman who didn't leave us by choice." She could no longer contain the sobs that ripped through her as the realization of the loss finally penetrated the veil of shock.

Charlie said nothing. He merely held tight as she cried for all she'd lost, for all she still might lose. She had always believed someplace deep in her heart that she would see her mother again, that somehow the wounds would be healed and they would love one another again.

That wasn't going to happen. Elizabeth couldn't rise up from the dead to spend even one precious instant with her children.

She cried until there was nothing left inside her and then, completely exhausted, she fell into blessed sleep.

"The initial finding is that she was probably strangled," Zack said to Charlie when he called the next morning. "Her larynx was crushed, and the coroner could find no other obvious signs of trauma. And there's no way she packed her own suitcases. The clothes inside were shoved in, not neatly folded. She was probably killed someplace else, then the suitcases were packed to make it appear that she'd left."

"And I suppose the suspect list is rather short," Charlie said dryly.

"Yeah, as in there isn't one." Zack's frustration was evident in his voice. "I've got the mayor chewing on my ass wanting answers as to what's happening in his town, and I don't have any answers to give him."

"I wish I could offer you some," Charlie replied.

"I interviewed both Lana and Leroy Racine last night. They remembered where they were on the day Elizabeth disappeared. Lana was in Oklahoma City getting her son a checkup with his physician and Leroy spent the day fishing. Other than that, I haven't had a chance to question anyone else. Hell, to be honest, I'm not even sure where to begin. I'm still trying to break Justin Walker's alibi for William's murder."

"You really think those kids killed him?" Charlie asked.

"I don't know what to think. I just collect the evidence and let the prosecuting attorney do the thinking. How's Grace doing this morning?"

"Still sleeping." And for that Charlie was grateful. He picked up his coffee from the table and took a sip. "Got any ideas about what's going on as far as the attacks on her?" he asked.

"I was hoping maybe you had some," Zack replied.

"I don't have a clue." Charlie frowned. It wasn't even nine o'clock and already his level of frustration was through the ceiling. "I don't suppose this new development changes anything with Hope's case?"

"A slick lawyer like you can probably make an argument that it should, but I don't think it will hold much weight. How do you tie a two-year-old murder into William's?"

Charlie blew out a deep breath. "I don't know, but in my gut I feel like they're all related—Elizabeth's and William's murders, Hope's incarceration and the attacks on Grace. Somehow they're connected, but I just can't get a handle on it."

"Well, if you do, I hope I'll be one of the first people you'll tell."

"And you'll let me know if anything new pops?"

"You got it," Zack replied.

Charlie hung up and stared out the window, his thoughts on the woman sleeping in the master bedroom. He was worried sick about her. She'd sat on the sofa in William's house like a stone statue, seemingly untouched by everything going on around her.

He'd always known she was a strong woman, but he'd known it wasn't strength that was keeping her so calm, so composed. Her brain had shut down, unable to handle any more trauma.

When the grief finally hit her, it had been horrible. Her sobs echoed in Charlie's heart, pulling forth his own grief for her. The worst part was knowing that he couldn't fix this for her. There was nothing he could say or do that would make her pain go away.

When she'd finally fallen asleep, exhausted by her river of tears, Charlie remained awake, his mind working overtime in an attempt to make sense of it all.

He could protect her from a gunman and make sure nobody could get at her without coming through him. But he couldn't protect her from grief, and that broke his heart.

Glancing at the clock, he was surprised to see that it was nearing ten. Grace never slept so late. He got up from the table and walked down the hallway to her purple bedroom, wanting to make sure she was okay.

She was awake but still in bed. "Hey," he said, and walked over to sit on the edge of the mattress. "How are you feeling?"

"As well as can be expected," she said. She sat up and pulled her legs up against her chest. Her eyes were slightly puffy from the tears, but Charlie thought she'd never looked as beautiful.

He reached out and smoothed a strand of her hair away from her face. She caught his hand and pressed it against her cheek. "I don't think I'm ready to face this day yet," she said softly.

"Then don't. There's nothing you need to do. If you want to stay in bed all day, nobody is going to complain. I'll even serve you your meals in here if you want me to," he said.

She smiled and reached up and pressed her mouth against his. He realized then that she must have gotten out of bed while he was on the phone with Zack, for her mouth tasted of minty toothpaste.

He tried to steel himself from the fire of desire that

instantly sprang to life inside him, but as she pulled him closer it was impossible to ignore.

A familiar ache of need began deep inside him, not just in his body but also in his heart. It was obvious what she wanted, and even though he knew he was a fool, it never entered his mind to deny her.

The kiss quickly became hot and hungry, and within seconds Charlie was naked and in bed with her. Last time, their lovemaking had been a slow renewal of old passion—a rediscovery between lovers—but now it was fast and hard and furious.

She encouraged him as he took her, her fingernails digging into his back, then into his buttocks. She cried out his name, whipping her head back and forth as she rocked beneath him.

He knew it was grief driving her to the wildness that possessed her. He held tight to her, as if to keep her from spinning off the face of the earth, and she cried out when she climaxed, a combination sob of pain and gasp of pleasure. He followed, losing it with a moan of her name.

Afterward he got up, grabbed his clothes and went into the bathroom to dress. Once again he felt a burgeoning anger swelling in his chest, and it was directed at Grace.

She had used him. He had the feeling that he could have been any man in her room just now. She'd just needed somebody and he was available.

She insisted she didn't want him and would never forgive him but pulled him into her bed and made him feel like he was the most important man in her world.

They needed to talk, but he was aware that now wasn't the time. She'd just lost her mother. She certainly wasn't in her right frame of mind, and he'd be a fool to attempt any meaningful conversation about the crazy relationship he now found himself in with her.

Just leave it alone, he told his reflection in the mirror. That's what a smart man would do. He drew a deep breath, sluiced water over his face and then did exactly what he'd told himself he wouldn't do.

"We need to talk," he said, when he returned to her bedroom.

Those beautiful blue eyes stared at him warily. "Talk about what?"

"About us, Grace. We need to talk about us." He refused to be put off by the vulnerable shine in her eyes.

She sighed, a tiny wrinkle appearing in the center of her forehead. "Do we really need to do this now?"

"We've put it off for eighteen months. I think we're past due for a conversation."

She raked a hand through her tousled hair. The sun drifting through the window caught and sparkled off her glorious golden strands.

His love for her blossomed so big in his chest he couldn't speak. How did you get into an unforgiving heart? How could he make her understand that he wasn't the same man he'd been in the past?

"Let me shower and have some coffee, then I guess we'll talk," she finally said with obvious dread in her voice.

He nodded and left her there with her hair shining

and her eyes filled with a sadness. He feared that he'd just made a huge mistake.

Grace stared at her reflection in the bathroom mirror. "What are you doing?" she asked the woman who stared back at her. "What are you doing making love with him when you hate him? Have you forgotten what he did to you?" No wonder he wanted to talk. She'd given him so many mixed signals it was ridiculous.

She whirled away from the mirror with a sigh of disgust. She'd let him get back into her heart. Somehow the drama of the past few days caused her to let down her guard.

She started the water in the shower and stepped in, hoping the stream would wash away the foolishness she'd entertained since he'd reentered her life and restore her to sanity.

When she'd come to him for help with Hope, she'd thought her anger and bitterness would shield her against any old feelings that might rear their head. But she hadn't expected his quiet support—his sensitivity to her every mood, his gentleness when she needed it most. She hadn't imagined his desire would be as fiery, as focused, as it had been before, and she certainly hadn't anticipated that he'd know when she needed a laugh.

She hadn't planned to fall in love with him all over again. She raised her face to the water, fighting against the new set of tears that burned her eyes. She couldn't go back. There was still a core of bitterness that remained inside her, an anger she refused to let go of for fear of being hurt again by him.

Stepping out of the shower, she grabbed a towel. She'd known this was coming. She'd known eventually they would talk about it. For weeks after she'd left him, he'd called, sent flowers and tried to communicate with her, but she hadn't given him a chance. The calls hadn't been answered and the flowers had gone directly into the trash.

Eventually he stopped reaching out to her, but there had never been any real closure between them. Now there would.

She dressed in a pair of bright yellow capris and a white and yellow blouse, hoping the sunny color would somehow bring warmth and comfort to her heart.

The one thing she couldn't think about was her mother. The grief would consume her. Her guilt would destroy her. It was better to stay focused on Charlie, to embrace the old rage that had once filled her where he was concerned.

She left her bedroom and found Charlie at the kitchen table. "The coffee is fresh," he said.

She nodded and poured herself a cup, then sat across from him, her fingers wrapped around the warmth of the drink. Grace was surprised to see a throbbing knot of tension in his jaw and the darkness of his charcoal eyes that looked remarkably like the first stir of anger.

"I can't imagine why you want to rake up the past," she finally said.

"Because it's there between us, because maybe if we talk about it, then you can finally let it go." He leaned back in his chair and studied her. "What I did was wrong, Grace. It was wrong on about a thousand different levels. Hell, I don't even remember that woman's name. I was drunk and she drove me home from the bar. It was a stupid thing for me to do, but I think we both need to accept some responsibility for what happened."

She sat up straighter in her chair and narrowed her eyes. "I certainly didn't encourage you to get stinking drunk and fall into bed with the first available woman." That old storm of anger whipped up inside her and the taste of betrayal filled her mouth.

"That's true and that's a mistake I'll always regret." A deep frown furrowed his forehead. "I'd won one of the biggest cases of my career that afternoon. Do you remember? I called you and wanted you to drive in, so we could celebrate, but you told me you had other plans for the weekend."

The heat of anger warmed her face. "So it's like the old song: if you can't be with the one you love, love the one you're with? If I wasn't available, it was okay for you to just find somebody else? That's not the way you have a loving, monogamous relationship."

"That was part of the problem," he exclaimed, a rising tension in his voice. "We never defined what, exactly, our relationship was. We never talked about it. We never discussed anything important."

He shoved back from the table with a force that surprised her and got up. "Hell, you didn't even tell me about your mother. You'd drive to my place twice a month for the weekend, but I didn't know what you did for the rest of the time. You never shared anything about your life here."

"And that makes it okay for you to cheat on me? Don't twist this around, Charlie. Don't make me the bad guy here." She embraced her anger, allowed it to fill her. It swept away the grief caused by her mother's death, the fear about Hope's future and the concern for her own personal safety.

He leaned a hip against the cabinets and shook his head. "I'm not trying to make you the bad guy. I'm trying to explain to you what my state of mind was that night. I was confused about you, about us."

"And while we were seeing each other how many other times were you confused?" Her voice was laced with sarcasm. "How many other women helped you clear your mind?"

"None," he said without hesitation. "You were always the one I wanted, but I never knew how you felt about me. I was afraid to tell you how I felt because I thought it would push you away." His voice was a low, husky rumble. "Tell the truth, Grace. I was just your good-time Charlie, available for a weekend of hot sex and laughs whenever you could work it into your schedule."

She stared at him in stunned surprise. "That wasn't the way it was, Charlie." Why was he twisting everything around and making it somehow feel like her fault? "Damn it, Charlie, that's not the way it was," she exclaimed.

He shoved his hands in his pockets and stared at her with dark, enigmatic eyes. "And the worst thing is we're back to where we started, only this time I'm your bad-time Charlie. Whenever you need somebody to hold you, to make love to you, you reach out to me because I'm the only man available."

She stood, her legs trembling with the force of her anger with him. She gripped the edge of the table with her hands. "You feel better, Charlie? You've managed to successfully turn your faults into mine. You've somehow absolved yourself of all guilt for cheating on me and made it all about my shortcomings. Congratulations," she added bitterly.

"I don't feel better. I feel sick inside." He reached up and swept a hand through his hair, and when he dropped his hand back to his side, his shoulders slumped in a way she'd never seen before. "I love you, Grace. I loved you then and I love you now and you've told me over and over again that you can't— or won't—forgive me. Well, I can't…. I won't make love to you again because it hurts too damn bad."

He turned on his heels and left the kitchen. A moment later she heard the sound of her guest-room door closing.

She sank back into the chair at the table, her legs no longer capable of holding her upright. This was what he did, she told herself. He twisted words and events to suit his own purposes. It was what made him a terrific defense attorney. It was why she'd contacted him to help with Hope's case.

He was an expert at making the guilty look innocent, at directing focus away from the matter at hand. He'd used those skills very well right now, but that didn't change the facts—didn't make his betrayal her fault.

Damn him. Damn him for telling her he loved her. And damn him for making her love him back. But just because she loved him didn't mean she intended to be a fool again.

He was right. She refused to forgive him, wouldn't take another chance on him. Her life was already in turmoil and that's what she had to focus on.

She had another funeral to plan. Her heart squeezed with a new pain as she thought of her mother. What she'd told Charlie about being friends with her mother was true.

They'd often met for lunch, and on most days Elizabeth would drop into the shop just to see what was new and spend some time with Grace. They'd shared the same sense of humor, the same kind of moral compass that made them easy companions.

So why had Grace been so quick to believe that her mother had done something so uncharacteristic as pack her bags and leave without a word? Instead of fostering her anger, she should have been out searching, beating every bush, overturning stones to find her mom. She should be thinking about Hope. God. She hated the fact that she was only allowed to see her at the detention center once a week. Hope was only able to call her every other day or so.

He loved her. The words jumped unbidden in her mind. Deep inside her, she'd known that he was in love with her. His feelings for her had been in his every touch, in the softness of his eyes, in the warmth of his arms whenever he'd comforted her.

And he was somewhat right about having been her good-time Charlie. When they'd met, she'd still been reeling from her mother's abandonment, and those weekends with him had been her escape from reality.

But why hadn't he seen that he'd been so much more than that to her? Why hadn't he recognized how much she'd loved him then? Maybe because she hadn't really shown him?

He was wrong about one thing. He was wrong to believe that when she made love with him he could have been anyone, that he just happened to be the man available. She'd wanted Charlie.

Grace felt as if she was born wanting Charlie, but that didn't mean she wanted to spend her life with him. That didn't mean she intended to forgive him and let him have a do-over with her.

They couldn't go on like they were, with him in her face every minute and in her bed whenever she wanted him.

It was time to let him go. She hoped he would still act as Hope's lawyer, but he couldn't be her bodyguard any longer. She'd have to make other arrangements.

It had been difficult to tell him goodbye the first time, but then she'd had her self-righteous anger to wrap around her like a cloak of armor. Now she had nothing but the realization that sometimes love just wasn't enough.

Chapter 12

Charlie walked out of the bedroom and back into the kitchen, but Grace wasn't there. She must have disappeared into her own room. He poured himself a cup of coffee and carried it to the window, where he stared outside.

How did you make a woman believe that you weren't the man you had once been? Losing Grace had shaken him to the very core, but it took his father's death to transform him.

His father hadn't liked the man he had become— a name-dropping, money-grabbing, slick lawyer who never managed to make time for the man who raised him.

Mark, Charlie's father, had called him often,

wanting him to come home and spend a little time at the ranch. Every holiday Mark had wanted Charlie home, but Charlie was always too busy. And then his dad was gone.

In the depths of his grief, Charlie came to realize his own unhappiness about the choices he'd made in his shallow life in the fast lane.

He'd recognized that what he truly wanted was to get back to the ranch, build a life of simple pleasures and hopefully share that life with a special woman.

When he fantasized about that woman, it was always Grace's face that filled his mind. He'd wanted her to be the one to share his life and give him children.

But it wasn't meant to be. There was no forgiveness in her heart, no room for him there. He turned away from the window as he heard the sound of heels on the floor.

He raised an eyebrow in surprise as he saw Grace, dressed in a cool blue power suit with white high heels and a white barrette clasped at the nape of her neck.

"I'm going into the shop for the day," she said. She walked over to where he stood and held out her hand. "Give me a dollar," she said.

He frowned. "What?"

"You heard me. Give me a dollar."

Charlie pulled his wallet from his back pocket, opened it and took one out. She took it from him and shoved it into the white purse she carried.

"I've just gotten my retainer back for your body-guard services. I'd still like you to continue with

Hope's case, but your services to me are no longer needed." Her cool blue eyes gave nothing away of her emotions.

"Are you crazy?" he exclaimed. "Have you forgotten that somebody is out to hurt you? Just because you can't trust or forgive me, isn't a good enough reason to put yourself at risk."

"I won't put myself at risk," she replied. "When I get to the shop, I'll give Dalton West a call and arrange for West Protective Services to keep an eye on me."

The idea of any other man being so intimately involved in her life definitely didn't sit well with him. Nobody would work harder than he at keeping Grace safe.

He set his cup down on the table. "Grace, for God's sake, don't let our personal issues force you to make a mistake. I can take care of you better than anyone."

She shook her head, her eyes dark with an emotion he couldn't discern. "I'm not making one. I feel like for the first time since William's murder I'm thinking clearly." She twisted the handle of her purse. "We can't go on like this, Charlie. It's too painful for both of us. I have enough things in my life to deal with right now without having to deal with you."

It surprised him that she still had the capacity to hurt him, but her words caused a dull ache to appear in the pit of his stomach.

"If you defend Hope, I'll pay you what I would pay any defense attorney," she continued. "And then we'll be square." She pulled her key ring from her purse. "I'd appreciate it if you're gone by the time I get home from the shop this evening."

"At least let me follow you to the shop," he said.

She hesitated and then nodded. "Okay."

He went back into the guest bedroom and packed what few things he'd brought with him. It wasn't until now that he realized how much he had hoped that they might be able to let go of the past and rebuild a new, better relationship.

Now, without that tenuous hope, he was empty. He carried his small bag down the hallway and found Grace waiting for him at the front door.

"Ready?" she asked. He noticed the slight tremble of her lower lip and realized this was just as difficult for her.

He nodded, and together they left the house. Charlie's car was in front of hers, the passenger window now intact. He walked her to her car door as his gaze automatically swept the area for any potential trouble.

When she was safely behind the steering wheel, he hurriedly got into his car. She pulled out of the driveway, and he followed her.

He could see her blond hair shining in the sunlight as they drove, that glorious hair that smelled vaguely of vanilla.

Again a painful ache swelled in his chest. He told himself it was good he got the opportunity to explain that terrible Friday night to her. He'd wanted her to know that he'd loved her despite what he had done.

Not that it mattered now.

He followed her down Main Street and parked in the space next to her. He was out of his car before she could get out of hers.

"I'll see you inside," he said, as he opened her car door.

He hovered at her back as she unlocked the shop and then they went in together. "I'll be fine now, Charlie," she said once she had the lights on and the Open sign in the window. "Nobody would be foolish enough to try to hurt me here during the middle of the day. People are in and out all day long."

He felt relatively confident that she was right. In the light of day in a fairly busy store, surely she'd be safe, but that didn't mean he intended to leave her safety to chance.

"You'll see to Hope?" she asked, and again her lower lip quivered as if she were holding back tears.

He nodded, the thick lump in his throat making him unable to speak for a moment.

"Charlie, thank you for everything you've done for me. I don't know how I would have gotten through the last week without you."

"I wish things could be different," he said, a last attempt at somehow reaching into her heart. "I wish you trusted that I'm different and realized how loving you is the biggest part of me."

Her eyes misted over and she stepped back to stand behind the cash register, as if needing a barrier between the two of them.

"Just go, Charlie." Her voice was a desperate plea. "Please just get out of here."

"Goodbye, Grace," he said softly, as he walked out the door and out of her life.

She watched him leave and had a ridiculous desire to run after him and tell him she didn't want him to go. Instead, she remained rooted in place as tears slowly ran from her eyes.

Angrily she wiped them away. It was better this way. They'd had their chance to make it work almost two years before and they'd blown it. Grace just wasn't willing to risk her heart again.

Stowing her purse beneath the counter, she tried not to think about the last time she'd been here.

Instead she went to the back room and dragged out a box of sandals that had come in so she could work on a new table display.

As she unpacked the cute, multicolored shoes, she tried to keep her mind off everything else. She needed a break. She desperately needed to not think about the murders or Hope and Charlie.

Here, in the confines of the shop, she'd always managed to clear her head by focusing on the simple pleasures of fabrics and textures. During those tough weeks after her mother disappeared, she'd found solace here. And when she and Charlie broke up, this place had been her refuge.

Today it didn't work. Nothing she did kept her mind off the very things she didn't want to think about. She had three customers in the morning and sold two pairs of the sandals she'd just put on display.

At noon she realized she hadn't made arrangements for lunch. Although the café was just up the street, she really didn't feel comfortable walking there alone. She should have packed a lunch, she thought, as she walked to the front window and peered outside.

She froze as she saw Charlie's car still parked next to hers. He was slumped down in the driver's seat but straightened up when he saw her in the window.

What did he think he was doing? They'd each said what needed to be said for closure. They'd said their goodbyes.

She opened the door, and before she could step out he scrambled from his car with the agility of a teenager. "What are you still doing here, Charlie?" she asked him, as he joined her at the door.

"It's a free country. I've got a right to sit in my car in a parking space on Main Street for as long as I want." He raised his chin with grim determination.

She narrowed her eyes. "What are you really doing?"

"Have you called West Protective Services yet?"

"Not yet. I was going to call after lunch."

"It's entirely up to you if you want to hire somebody else, but that doesn't mean I'm going to stop watching over you. I can guard you better than anyone you can hire, Grace, because I care about you more than anyone else. Don't worry, I don't intend to be an intrusion. There's really no way you can stop me short of getting a restraining order."

He'd often accused her of being stubborn, but she saw the thrust of his chin, the fierce determination in his eyes, and she knew it would be pointless to argue with him.

"Fine," she said, a weary resignation sweeping over her. "You can go now."

"What are you doing for lunch?" he asked.

"I'm not really hungry," she lied.

"Okay, then I'll just go back to being a shadow," he replied. He left her standing at the door and went back to his car.

She returned to her position behind the cash register and sat, trying to forget that she now had a shadow she didn't want and a heartache she knew would stay with her for a very long time.

Thirty minutes later her "shadow" reappeared in the store with a foam container from the café. He set it on the counter in front of her without saying a word, then walked out the front door.

Her stomach growled as she opened the lid. A cheeseburger was inside, its aroma filling the air and making her stomach rumble. She pulled off the top bun and saw just mustard and a pickle. Onions were on the side.

He'd remembered. After all this time, he still knew exactly how she liked her burgers. And it was this fact that broke her.

Tears blurred her vision as she stared at the burger and a deep sob ripped out of her. This time she knew what her tears were for. They were for lost love…they were for Charlie.

She only managed to pull herself together when the door opened and Rachel came in. "I just heard," she exclaimed, and immediately wrapped her arms around Grace's shoulders.

For one crazy moment, Grace thought she was talking about Charlie, but then she realized Rachel must have heard about her mother, and that made her tears come faster and harder.

All the losses she'd suffered over the last week came crashing back in on her. "Come on, let's go into the back," Rachel said. Grace locked the front door and allowed Rachel to lead her to the office. Grace sat at her desk and Rachel pulled a chair around a stack of boxes to sit next to her.

Grace grabbed a handful of tissues from a nearby box and dabbed at her eyes. "I've been so angry at her. I hated her for leaving and now I learn she's been dead this whole time."

"Does the sheriff have any leads?"

Grace shook her head. "None. Charlie thinks it might all be related, Mom's murder and William's." She began to cry. "Oh Rachel, I've made a mess of things. I've fallen in love with Charlie again."

"Grace, who are you fooling? You never stopped loving him," Rachel replied. "I saw him outside sitting in his car. What's really going on between the two of you?"

"Nothing now. Nothing anymore. He's just keeping an eye on me because of the attack the other night. And I want him to defend Hope when her case comes to trial." Grace decided not to go into the whole story about the shooting and how somebody was trying to kill her. "He says he loves me, that he always has."

"What are you going to do about it?" Rachel asked.

Grace sighed. "Nothing. I do think he's changed, Rachel. I believe that he's a different man than he was before, but I still have a knot of anger that I can't seem to get past where he's concerned."

"There are other good defense attorneys, Grace. If you really want to put him in your past, if you really have no desire to have anything to do with him, then find another attorney for Hope. Get Charlie Black completely out of your life."

Those words haunted Grace long after Rachel left the store. Grace ate the cold burger and considered her alternatives. She knew she should do what Rachel suggested, but she told herself that she wasn't convinced any other lawyer would work as hard as Charlie to defend Hope.

The afternoon was busier than usual. Prom was in less than a month, and more than a few high school girls came in to try on the sparkly gowns Grace carried just for the occasion.

When there weren't any customers in the store, Grace drifted by the window, oddly comforted by the fact that Charlie remained in his car.

"It's like having my own personal stalker," she muttered with dark humor at seven o'clock, as she turned the Open sign to Closed and locked the door.

She carried the cash register drawer to the back office to close out and sank down into the chair at the desk.

She was tired but didn't want to go home. Tonight she would be alone, without Charlie. She assumed he'd probably sleep in his car in her driveway, and while the idea that he would be uncomfortable bothered her, she would not allow her emotions to manipulate her into inviting him back in.

Let him go completely. A little voice whispered inside her head. *Or grab him with both hands and hold tight.* It has to be one or the other.

Because there had been more sales than usual during the day, it took her longer than normal to close out the books. It was almost eight by the time she locked up her desk. Still she was reluctant to leave.

She stood and stretched with her arms overhead and eyed the stack of boxes next to her desk. She should spend another hour or two unpacking the new products. There was a box of swimwear and another of beach towels and matching totes.

It wouldn't be long before summer was upon them. Where would Hope be this summer? Would she still be locked up in the detention center awaiting her trial, or would some evidence be found that would bring her home before the dog days of summer?

She would need to be mother and father to Hope now. She wouldn't be able to spend long hours here. She'd need to be available for her sister, to guide and love her.

As much as she loved the store, she loved her sister more. Dana could take on more responsibility and Grace could be what Hope needed, what she wanted.

She pulled the top box off the tall stack, moved it to her desk and opened it. It would take her about an hour to tag all the swimwear, and then she'd go home.

As she worked, she kept her mind as empty of thought as possible. It was just after nine when she finished. She was just about to leave her office when she heard a knock on the back door.

Who on earth…? She walked to the door and hesitated with her hand on the lever that would disarm the security alarm. "Who is it?" she yelled through the door.

"Grace, it's me, Leroy Racine. I need to talk to you. I remembered something…something about the night before William was murdered."

Was it possible this was the break they had been looking for? Grace disarmed the door and opened it partway to look at the big man. In the dark, she could barely discern his features. "What are you talking about?"

"The night before William's murder he had a visitor, a business associate of some kind. I was outside working, but I heard them yelling at each other."

Grace's heart leapt with excitement as she opened the door to allow him inside. "Come on into my office," she said, and gestured him into the chair where Rachel had sat earlier in the day.

Leroy sank into the chair and Grace sat at her desk. "I don't know why I didn't remember this before," he said.

"So, exactly what is it that you've remembered?"

Grace asked. She leaned forward, hoping, praying that whatever information Leroy had would point the finger of guilt away from Hope and to the real killer.

"It's really not what I've remembered as much as it is what I need to finish." He pulled a wicked, gleaming knife and leaned forward, so close to her that she could feel the heat of his breath on her face. "Tomorrow everyone will talk about how the robber who got away the other night came back here, only this time with tragic results. Don't scream, Grace, don't even move."

Leroy? Her mind struggled to make sense of what was happening. Grace stared into his dark eyes and knew she was in trouble, the kind of trouble people didn't survive.

Zack West's car pulled up beside Charlie's, and the lawman stepped out and walked up to his window. "Everything all right? You've been parked here for the whole day."

Charlie opened his car door and stepped out, his kinked muscles protesting the long hours in the car. "I'm just waiting for Grace to call it a day so I can follow her home." He shot a glance toward the darkened storefront. "I think she's working late on purpose just to aggravate me." He leaned against the side of his car and frowned. "Why are women so damned complicated?"

Zack laughed. "I don't know. I certainly don't always understand Kate, and we've been married for a while now." Zack headed back to his car. "I just wanted to make sure everything was all right here."

"Everything is fine," Charlie assured him. "I'm hoping she's going to call it a night pretty quickly, so I can get her home safe and sound."

Zack nodded, then got back into his car and pulled away. Charlie folded his arms and gazed at the shop.

How much longer was she going to be? He wouldn't put it past her to be cooling her heels intentionally, knowing he was sitting out here waiting for her.

Charlie had already made arrangements with Dalton West to help him keep an eye on her. Once Grace was back in her house, Dalton would take over surveillance on her place while Charlie went home and grabbed a shower and a couple of hours of sleep.

By the time Grace woke up the next morning, Charlie would once again be on duty for the day. He didn't care what she said. He wasn't going to leave her unprotected until they figured out exactly what in the hell was going on.

Eventually he'd need to figure out a way to cast her not only out of his thoughts, but out of his heart as well.

He checked his watch, then got back into his car and leaned his head back, waiting for her to call it a night.

Chapter 13

"Leroy, what are you doing?" Grace's voice was laced with the terror that coursed through her. She stared at him, trying to make sense of what was going on.

"What am I doing?" He smiled then, a proud, boastful smile. "I'm completing a plan that's been ten years in the making."

"What does that mean?" Grace slid her eyes toward the top of her desk, looking for something she could use as a weapon. Inside the drawer was a box cutter and a pair of scissors, but on top there was nothing more lethal than a ballpoint pen.

Leroy's eyes glittered darkly and he leaned forward, as if eager to share with her whatever was going on in his head. "It started when I met Lana and found out she was carrying William Covington's baby."

Grace gasped and stared at him incomprehensively. "What are you talking about? Lincoln is only ten years old. William and my mother were married at the time he was conceived. William wouldn't have cheated on my mother."

Leroy laughed, but there was nothing pleasant in the sound. "Ah, but he did. Your mother had flown to Las Vegas to help out one of her friends who was having a difficult pregnancy. Remember? She was gone for two weeks, and on one of those nights William and my lovely wife crossed the line. It only happened once, but that was enough for her to wind up pregnant."

She reeled with the information. Lana and William? What Leroy said might be true, but it still didn't illuminate everything that had happened over the last week and a half.

The fact that he hadn't lowered the knife and still held it tightly in his hand as if ready to thrust it into her at any moment kept a lump of fear firmly lodged in her throat.

If she screamed, he could gut her before anyone would hear her cry for help. She thought of Charlie in his car out front and wanted to weep because she had no way of letting him know she was in danger.

"What do you want, Leroy? Money? I have my cash drawer in the desk. Just let me unlock it and I'll give you everything I have."

"Oh Grace, I definitely want money, but I'm not interested in whatever you have in that drawer," he replied. "I've been a very patient man and soon my patience is all going to pay off." He must have seen the look of confusion on her face for he laughed once again. "William's money, Grace. That's what I'm after. Lincoln is a Covington heir—and why should he share an inheritance when he can have it all."

Grace had been afraid before, but as the realization of his words penetrated her frightened fog, a new sense of terror gripped her. "You killed William? It was you? And you set up Hope to take the fall."

Again a proud grin lifted the corner of Leroy's mouth. "It was genius. Your sister, she's a creature of habit. Every morning she makes herself breakfast and drinks about a half a gallon of orange juice. That girl loves her juice."

"You drugged it," Grace exclaimed.

"It was brilliant. She went back to bed and passed out. I killed William, trashed her room, smeared her with blood and put the knife in her hand. And before she goes to trial I'll make sure the prosecutor has all the evidence he needs to send her away for the rest of her life."

"I don't understand any of this," Grace cried, tears misting her vision as she tried to buy time. "Did you kill my mother, too?"

Leroy leaned back in the chair, but the knife never wavered. "Apparently William decided to come clean to your mother about that night with Lana. The next morning your mother came to the cottage wanting to talk to Lana, but she'd taken Lincoln into Oklahoma City for a doctor's appointment. You see, for me to make sure my stepson inherited all of William's money, I needed to make sure nobody else was going to inherit it. Your mother was the first obstacle in the way. I strangled her, and since nobody was home at the mansion, I packed a couple of her suitcases to make it look like she took off."

Grace closed her eyes as grief battled with terror inside her. Reward. Charlie had been trying to figure out the true motive of William's murder and now she knew. Money. William's money. Leroy wanted it all not for Lincoln, but for himself. With Lincoln being underage, Leroy and Lana would be in charge of the fortune.

What did Lana know? Was she a part of this? God, it would be the final betrayal to learn that the loving housekeeper had helped plot all these murders.

Grace opened her eyes and realized she was going to die here now if she didn't do something.

"I had to bide my time after your mother died. I knew I couldn't take out William too quickly or people would be suspicious," he said.

"People *are* suspicious," she said, barely able to hear her own voice over the pounding of her heartbeat. "You'll never get away with this, Leroy. When you try to collect William's money, the suspicions will only get bigger."

"Suspecting and proving are two different things.

William's murder is going to be pinned on Hope. Your mother's murder happened two years ago, and by the time I plant bugs in some people's ears it will all make perfect sense."

His dark eyes gleamed bright. "You see, the way the story will go is that your mother found out about William's night with Lana and was going to leave him. They fought and things got out of control and he killed her. Two years later, Hope began to suspect what had happened and believing that William was responsible for your mother's death, she killed him. And you, you're just the tragic victim of a store robbery. Nobody can tie up all the pieces so they point in my direction. You'll all be gone and a DNA test will prove Lincoln to be a rightful heir."

Grace knew she was running out of time. She had to do something to escape or at least to draw attention. Once again her gaze shot around, looking for anything that might help her.

The stacked boxes next to where he sat caught her eye. She tensed all her muscles, knowing it was very possible she'd die trying to escape him, but she would certainly be killed if she did nothing.

Now or never, she told herself as Leroy continued bragging about how smart he'd been to pull off everything. *Now or never,* the words screamed through her head.

She exploded from the chair and knocked down the stack of boxes. They toppled on top of Leroy as she ran for the door of the office, sobs of terror ripping out of her.

The sales floor was dark, lit only by the faint security lights and the dim illumination coming through the front window. She focused on the door. If she could just get out, Charlie would be there and everything would be all right.

She made it as far as the table display of sandals before she was tackled from behind. They both tumbled to the floor. Shoes fell on top of them as they bumped against the table.

Leroy cursed and momentarily let go of her. Frantically Grace crawled on her hands and knees into the middle of a circular rack of blouses, swallowing her sobs in an effort to hide from him.

If she screamed for Charlie, she would pinpoint her location to Leroy, who apparently hadn't seen exactly where she had gone. Even if Charlie heard her scream, she was afraid he wouldn't be able to get inside before Leroy killed her.

She could smell the man, the sour scent of sweat. She could hear him moving around the store, hunting her like a predator stalking prey.

Her body began a tremble she feared would move the blouses. Drawing deep, silent breaths, she tried to control the fear that threatened to erupt. She tensed as she heard Leroy's footsteps getting closer…closer still.

"Grace, you're just prolonging the inevitable," he said softly. The rack of blouses shook and despite her desire to stay silent, a slight whimper escaped her as she realized he knew where she was hiding.

She had to scream and she had to move. It was the only way Charlie might hear her and get out of his car to check it out.

At that moment, the knife slashed through the rack of blouses and a scream ripped out of her.

Charlie drummed his fingers on the steering wheel in time to the beat of the music from his radio. He was beginning to wonder if Grace was going to spend the entire night in the store.

Main Street had emptied of cars long ago, and most of the townspeople were now in their homes, watching television or getting ready for bed.

Charlie would love to be getting ready for bed, especially if Grace was waiting in it. He couldn't help but think of the last two times they made love and how he would happily spend the rest of his life loving her and only her.

What was keeping her from him? There had been moments over the past week when he hadn't felt the burden of their past between them and thought she'd gotten past her bitterness. He'd felt her love for him and entertained a tiny flicker of hope that there might be a future for them together.

He rubbed a hand across his forehead, weary with the inactivity of the day and thoughts of Grace. It was done. There was no point in trying to figure out what went wrong this time. Apparently she'd never really gotten over their past and refused to even consider any future with him.

He frowned as he saw a shadow move across the

plate glass window in front of the shop. Sitting up straighter, he breathed a grateful sigh. Good, maybe she was getting ready to go home.

He got back out of the car and stretched with his arms overhead, then shoved his hands in his pockets and waited for her to walk out the front door.

Again he saw shadowy movement inside the store and heard a noise—a scream. Alarm rang in his head as he yanked his hands from his pockets and ran to the front door. Locked.

"Grace?" he yelled and banged on the door with his fists. Wild with fear as he saw not one figure, but two, he looked around frantically, needing something he could use to break the door down.

He spied a heavy flowerpot in front of the store-front next door. As soon as he grabbed it, he threw it at the window.

The pot went through with a crash and the entire window cracked and shattered. Before the glass had cleared enough for him to get inside, Grace opened the front door.

She was sobbing and held an arm that was bleeding. "It's Leroy," she cried. "Leroy Racine. He ran out the back door. Charlie, he killed them. He killed them all and he tried to kill me."

"Get in my car and lock the doors," he said, refusing to look at her bloody arm. He was filled with an all-consuming rage. "Call Zack. My cell phone is on the passenger seat."

He pulled his gun and took off around the side of the building, knowing Leroy had to be using the alley for his escape. Leroy? As Charlie ran, a million questions raced through his head.

Leroy was a big man, not as fast on his feet as Charlie, and on the next block from Grace's shop he spied the man rounding a corner.

Charlie had never wanted to catch a man more in his life. As he raced, his head filled with visions of Grace being hit over the head with an object, of her being kicked in the ribs. The rage that ripped through him knew no bounds. He wanted to kill Leroy Racine, but first he wanted to beat the hell out of him.

"Stop or I'll shot," Charlie yelled, as he saw Leroy just ahead of him. "I swear to God, Racine, I'll shoot you in the back and not blink an eye."

Leroy must have recognized the promise in Charlie's voice, for he stopped running and turned toward him, a frantic defeat spread across his face.

At that moment the whine of a siren sounded in the distance, and Charlie knew Zack or one of his deputies was responding to Grace's call.

"Get down on the ground," Charlie commanded. "Facedown on the ground with your hands up over your head."

Leroy hesitated but must have seen something in Charlie's eyes that frightened him, for he complied. Charlie kicked the knife Leroy held in one hand and sent it spinning several feet away. He leaned over him and pressed the barrel of his gun into the back of Leroy's head.

"Don't try anything," he warned the big man. "Don't even blink too hard. One way or the other you're going away for a very long time. It's either going to be jail or hell."

At that moment Zack ran toward them, his gun drawn and his eyes wide as he saw Charlie. "He killed Elizabeth and William, set up Hope to go to prison and tried to kill Grace." Charlie's voice grew hoarse with anger. "His knife is over there."

"Charlie, you can step away from him," Zack said, his voice deceptively calm. "I've got him now."

Reluctantly, Charlie pulled his gun from the back of Leroy's head and straightened. Before anyone could stop him, he drew back his boot and delivered a swift kick to Leroy's ribs.

Leroy yelped and raised his head to look at Zack. "Did you see that? I want him arrested for assault."

Charlie looked at Zack, who shrugged. "I didn't see anything," Zack replied.

"I've got to check on Grace. She was hurt," Charlie said, as Zack pulled Leroy to his feet and cuffed him.

Charlie took off running in the direction he'd come from. He still didn't have any real answers, couldn't figure out why Leroy had done what he'd done, but at the moment answers didn't matter—only Grace did.

She saw him coming and got out of his car. In the light from the nearby street lamp, he could see that her cheeks were shiny with tears, and she held her arm against her side, one hand pressed against the opposite upper arm.

"Charlie," she cried, as he neared. "Thank God you're okay."

He reached her and pulled her gently into his arms, careful not to hurt her.

As he smelled the familiar scent of vanilla in her hair and felt the warmth of her body against his, Charlie did something he couldn't remember doing since he was a young boy and his mother had died—he wept.

It was nearing dawn when Charlie followed Grace home. The night had been endless for Grace. At the hospital, she'd received eight stitches in her arm and then spent most of the rest of the night with Zack, telling him everything Leroy had told her.

She was beyond exhaustion yet elated. Zack promised her that first thing in the morning he'd get the wheels of justice turning to release Hope.

Hope was coming home, and it was time to tell Charlie a final goodbye. When they reached her house, she pulled into the driveway and parked. Charlie pulled in just behind her.

She didn't have to be afraid anymore. She could get out of her car without waiting for Charlie and his gun to protect her. She no longer needed him as a private investigator, a criminal defense attorney or a bodyguard. It was time for them to move on with their lives.

She got out of the car with weariness weighing on her shoulders and the whisper of something deeper, something that felt remarkably like new heartbreak.

Charlie joined her on the sidewalk and silently walked with her to her front door. "You're going to be all right now, Grace," he said.

She unlocked the door and then turned back to face him. His features looked haggard in the dawn light, and she fought her impulse to reach up and lay her palm against his cheek. "Yes, I'm going to be all right," she replied softly.

"Hope should be released sometime tomorrow, and the two of you can begin rebuilding your lives." He reached a hand up, as if to tuck a strand of her hair behind her ear, but instead he quickly dropped his hand back to his side. "You don't have any reason to be afraid anymore. It's finally over."

She nodded, surprised by the rise of a lump in her throat. He stared at her, and in the depths of his beautiful gray eyes, she saw his want, his need of her and she steeled herself against it, against him.

"Then I guess this is goodbye," he said, although it was more a question, a plea than a statement.

Her chest felt tight, constricted by her aching heart. "Goodbye, Charlie." She said the words quickly, then escaped into the house and closed the door behind her. She leaned against the door and felt the hot press of tears at her eyes.

She should have been happy. The bad times were behind her, so why was she crying? Why did she feel as if she'd just made the biggest mistake of her life?

Chapter 14

"It's just a movie, Grace," Hope said plaintively. "We'll go straight to the theater, and when the movie is over, we'll come right back here."

Grace took a sip of her coffee and frowned at her sister. It had been a week since Hope had gotten out of the detention center and moved into Grace's house.

The spare bedroom was now filled with all things teenage. Grace welcomed the chaos, the laughter and the drama that had filled the last seven days of her life.

Hope's release wasn't the only positive thing that happened over the last week. Although Lana had been devastated to learn that the man she'd married had done so only for the sake of Lincoln's inheritance, the knowledge that he'd murdered William and Elizabeth had nearly destroyed her.

She'd come to Grace begging for forgiveness, both for the horrific things her husband had done and for her own mistake in sleeping with William on that single night.

She'd explained that William had been missing Elizabeth desperately and invited her to have a drink with him. One drink led to half a dozen and suddenly they were both making the biggest mistake of their lives.

She hadn't told William that she'd gotten pregnant. She met Leroy a month later, and when she gave birth William assumed, like everyone else, that Lincoln was Leroy's child.

Grace assured her there was nothing to forgive and made Lana promise that she would allow Grace and Hope to get to know Lincoln, who would share in the inheritance that William had left behind.

"Earth to Grace." Hope's voice penetrated Grace's thoughts. "So can I go to a movie with Justin or not?"

Grace sighed, wishing this parenting stuff was easier. "I don't know, Hope."

Hope reached across the table and took Grace's hand in hers. "Grace, I know Justin has made some stupid mistakes in his past, like dropping out of high school, but he's really a nice guy. He deserves another chance."

"You'll go right to the theater and come right back here?" Grace asked.

"Pinky swear," Hope replied, lacing her pinky finger with Grace's.

"Okay. We'll consider this a test run."

"Cool." Hope was out of the chair almost before the words had left Grace's mouth. "I've got to call him and tell him I can go."

As she ran for her bedroom, Grace leaned back in her chair and sighed. This would be the first time Hope would be out of her sight since coming home.

Maybe part of her reluctance in letting Hope go was because Grace didn't want to spend the evening alone. Being alone always brought thoughts of Charlie and a sadness that felt never ending.

She hadn't seen him in the past week, but every time she got beneath the sheets on her bed she saw him in her mind, felt him in her heart.

Forgetting Charlie was proving more difficult than she'd thought. She got up from the table and carried her coffee cup to the sink, then stood by the window and stared out into the backyard.

He'd accused her of holding back, of confusing him when they'd been dating. She remembered the night he'd called her, so excited by his big win in court that day, asking her—no, begging her—to drive in to celebrate with him.

The sheer force of her desire to be with him had frightened her, and she'd told him she couldn't make it. Hours later she'd changed her mind and decided to surprise him. Unfortunately she was the one who had gotten the biggest surprise.

Hope walked back into the kitchen. "It's all set. Justin will pick me up at seven."

Grace turned from the window and forced a smile. "And you told him you needed to be home right after?"

"Yeah, but I was thinking maybe after the movie Justin could come in and we could bake a frozen pizza or something. I think if you talk to him for a while, you know, get to really know him, then you'll like him."

"That sounds like a nice idea," Grace replied.

Hope walked over to stand next to Grace and looked out the window. "When Mom left, I thought nobody else would ever care about me," Hope said softly. "I figured if my own mother didn't like me enough to stick around, why would anyone else like me?"

Grace put her arm around Hope's slender shoulders. "I know. I felt the same way."

"But, then I met Justin and even though he had a reputation as a tough guy, he made me feel better. He told me I was pretty and nice and that it was Mom's problem, not me, that drove her away."

"And now we know that she didn't leave us at all," Grace replied.

They were silent for a few minutes, and Grace knew they were both thinking of the mother they had buried two days before.

Hope finally looked at her. "It's important to me that you give Justin a chance, Grace. You don't have to worry about him taking advantage of me, or anything like that. Justin knows I want to stay a virgin for a long time and he's cool with that."

"I promise I'll give him a chance," Grace replied.

Hope reached up and kissed Grace on the cheek. "I'm going to go take a shower and get ready. Seven o'clock will be here before I know it."

Once again she left the kitchen and Grace turned her gaze back out the window. She could definitely relate to those feelings Hope described, of believing that if her mother didn't love her enough to stick around that nobody else would really love her.

She'd carried that emotion into her relationship with Charlie, and despite her deep feelings for him, she'd kept a big part of herself walled off from him, certain that eventually he'd leave her, too. She had to be unworthy of love because her mother had found her so.

Charlie told her she needed to accept partial responsibility for the demise of their relationship, and he was right.

She had treated him like a good-time Charlie, flying into his life for fun and laughs but never sharing with him any piece of herself, of her life here in Cotter Creek.

No wonder he hadn't seen their relationship in the same way she had. She'd given him so many mixed signals.

And now it was too late for her, for them.

Charlie sat on the back of his favorite stallion and gazed at the fencing he'd spent the last week repairing. It had been grueling physical work, but he'd welcomed it because it kept his mind off Grace.

He hadn't even gone into town during the past week. When he needed supplies, he sent one of his ranch hands in to get them. Charlie hadn't wanted to run into Grace or even see her storefront.

He wondered if everyone had that one love who stayed with you until the day you died and haunted you with a bittersweet wistfulness.

Leaning down, he patted his horse's neck, then grabbed the reins and turned around to head back to the house. It was too bad there wasn't a pill he could take that would banish all thoughts of Grace Covington from his mind. He was just going to have to live with his regrets and the overwhelming ache of what might have been.

Just then, as he approached the corral, Charlie saw the car pull into his driveway. Her car. His heart leapt, then calmed as he cautioned himself with wariness.

Maybe something else had happened—a legal issue she wanted help with or a question that needed to be answered. As he dismounted from the horse, she stepped out of her car, the fading sunlight sparking on her glorious hair and tightening the lump that rose up in his chest.

She looked lovely in a turquoise and white sundress, with turquoise sandals on her feet and a matching purse slung over her shoulder.

She couldn't keep doing this, he thought, as he walked slowly toward where she stood. She had to stop using him as her go-to man.

"Grace, what's up?" he asked, his tone curt.

She leaned against her car door. "Hope just left to go to a movie with Justin."

He frowned. "And you drove all the way out here to tell me that? Gee, thanks for the info, but I'm not sure why I need to know that." He stuffed his hands in his pockets, afraid that if he allowed them to wander free he'd reach out and run a finger across her full lower lip.

"Earlier this evening Hope and I had a chat about our mother and how she felt when we thought she'd abandoned us. She told me she thought nobody would ever love her again, and I realized that's exactly how I'd felt."

She pushed off from the door, her eyes dark and so sad that Charlie felt her sadness resonating in his own heart. "I hope both of you feel better about things now that you know the truth," he said.

"I don't feel better," she exclaimed and her eyes grew shiny with tears. "Oh Charlie, you were right about me. I did use you, but somewhere along the line I fell in love with you."

"And then I got drunk and stupid and screwed it all up," he replied, as a hollow wind blew through him. "We've been through all this, Grace."

He sighed with a weariness that etched deep into his soul. "I can keep Hope out of jail for a crime she didn't commit and I can probably keep you safe from some crazy stalker, but I don't know how to get you to trust me again."

She took several steps closer to him and that amazing scent of hers stirred the desire he would always feel for her. Still he kept his hands firmly tucked into his pockets, not wanting a moment of weakness to allow him to touch her in any way.

"I swore I didn't believe in second chances, that only a fool would give a man her heart again after he'd broken it once." Again her eyes took on the sheen of barely suppressed tears. "And then I realized I'd never really given you my heart for safe-keeping the first time. How could you know you were breaking it when you didn't realize it was yours?"

Charlie stared at her, afraid to believe what he thought her words might mean. "Why are you here, Grace?"

"I'm here because I realize I'm a different person now than I was when we were dating. And if I can believe that I'm a different person, then why can't I believe that you are? I'm here because for the first time in a year and a half I don't have my anger at you to fill me up, to protect me. And without that anger all I'm left with is my love for you."

Tears fell from her eyes and splashed onto her cheeks. "I'm here to find out if it's too late for me…for us."

Charlie's heart swelled so big in his chest he couldn't speak. He yanked his hands out of his pockets and opened his arms to her.

She fell into his embrace and he held her tight, feeling as if he were complete for the very first time. The scent of vanilla and jasmine smelled like home. Grace smelled like home.

"Charlie?" She raised her face to look at him. "It's not just me anymore. I'm a package deal. Hope is and will always be a part of my life."

"I always wanted a sister-in-law," he replied.

"Sister-in-law?" Grace stared at him, and that sweet lower lip of hers trembled. "Is that some kind of a crazy proposal, Charlie?"

He dropped his hands to his sides and smiled at her. "Give me a dollar."

"What?"

"You heard me, give me one." He held out his hand.

She opened her purse and pulled out a dollar bill. He took it from her and shoved it into his back pocket. "You've now retained the lifelong services of a criminal defense attorney and bodyguard." He pulled her into his arms, his gaze warm and soft, relaxed. "Better yet, you've got my love through eternity."

She returned to his embrace. "All that for a dollar? You're cheap, Charlie."

He grinned at her. "Only for the woman I love." His smile faded and he gazed at her intently. "Marry me, Grace. Marry me and be my wife. Share my life with me."

Charlie's words filled Grace with a kind of happiness that she'd never before experienced. This was right, she thought. This was the first right thing that had happened in a very long time, and she had no doubt that it would last forever.

"Yes, Charlie, I want to marry you. I want you to be my good-time Charlie, my bad-time Charlie, my forever Charlie."

He kissed her then, a hungry yet tender kiss that

held both the regrets of the past and the promise of the future. He wasn't the only one with regrets. Grace knew that their future together might have begun sooner if she'd been less afraid of putting her heart on the line when they'd been dating.

"Better late than never," she murmured, as their kiss finally ended.

"Second chances, Grace. Sometimes that's all we need." His eyes glowed with a light that always weakened her knees and curled her toes. "How long does that movie last?"

She grinned. "Long enough," she exclaimed, and grabbed his hand. Together they ran for the ranch house where his bed and their future awaited.

* * * * *

*Celebrate 60 years of pure
reading pleasure with Harlequin®!
Silhouette® Romantic Suspense is celebrating
with the glamour-filled, adrenaline-charged series
LOVE IN 60 SECONDS
starting in April 2009.
Six stories that promise to bring the glitz
of Las Vegas, the danger of revenge,
the mystery of a missing diamond,
family scandals and ripped-from-the-headlines
intrigue. Get your heart racing as
love happens in sixty seconds!*

Enjoy a sneak peek of
USA TODAY *bestselling author
Marie Ferrarella's*
THE HEIRESS'S 2-WEEK AFFAIR
*Available April 2009
from Silhouette® Romantic Suspense.*

Eight years ago Matt Shaffer had vanished out of Natalie Rothchild's life, leaving behind a one-line note tucked under a pillow that had grown cold: *I'm sorry, but this just isn't going to work.*

That was it. No explanation, no real indication of remorse. The note had been as clinical and compassionless as an eviction notice, which, in effect, it had been, Natalie thought as she navigated through the morning traffic. Matt had written the note to evict her from his life.

She'd spent the next two weeks crying, breaking down without warning as she walked down the street, or as she sat staring at a meal she couldn't bring herself to eat.

Candace, she remembered with a bittersweet pang, had tried to get her to go clubbing in order to get her to forget about Matt.

She'd turned her twin down, but she did get her act together. If Matt didn't think enough of their relationship to try to contact her, to try to make her understand why he'd changed so radically from lover to stranger, then to hell with him. He was dead to her, she resolved. And he'd remained that way.

Until twenty minutes ago.

The adrenaline in her veins kept mounting.

Natalie focused on her driving. Vegas in the daylight wasn't nearly as alluring, as magical and glitzy as it was after dark. Like an aging woman best seen in soft lighting, Vegas's imperfections were all visible in the daylight. Natalie supposed that was why people like her sister didn't like to get up until noon. They lived for the night.

Except that Candace could no longer do that.

The thought brought a fresh, sharp ache with it.

"Damn it, Candy, what a waste," Natalie murmured under her breath.

She pulled up before the Janus casino. One of the three valets currently on duty came to life and made a beeline for her vehicle.

"Welcome to the Janus," the young attendant said cheerfully as he opened her door with a flourish.

"We'll see," she replied solemnly.

As he pulled away with her car, Natalie looked up at the casino's logo. Janus was the Roman god with two faces, one pointed toward the past, the other facing the future. It struck her as rather ironic, given what she was doing here, seeking out someone from her past in order to get answers so that the future could be settled.

The moment she entered the casino, the Vegas phenomena took hold. It was like stepping into a world where time did not matter or even make an appearance. There was only a sense of "now."

Because in Natalie's experience she'd discovered that bartenders knew the inner workings of any establishment they worked for better than anyone else, she made her way to the first bar she saw within the casino.

The bartender in attendance was a gregarious man in his early forties. He had a quick, sexy smile, which was probably one of the main reasons he'd been hired. His name tag identified him as Kevin.

Moving to her end of the bar, Kevin asked, "What'll it be, pretty lady?"

"Information." She saw a dubious look cross his brow. To counter that, she took out her badge. Granted she wasn't here in an official capacity, but Kevin didn't need to know that. "Were you on duty last night?"

Kevin began to wipe the gleaming black surface of the bar. "You mean during the gala?"

"Yes."

The smile gracing his lips was a satisfied one. Last night had obviously been profitable for him, she judged. "I caught an extra shift."

She took out Candace's photograph and carefully

placed it on the bar. "Did you happen to see this woman there?"

The bartender glanced at the picture. Mild interest turned to recognition. "You mean Candace Rothchild? Yeah, she was here, loud and brassy as always. But not for long," he added, looking rather disappointed. There was always a circus when Candace was around, Natalie thought. "She and the boss had at it and then he had our head of security escort her out."

She latched onto the first part of his statement. "They argued? About what?"

He shook his head. "Couldn't tell you. Too far away for anything but body language," he confessed.

"And the head of security?" she asked.

"He got her to leave."

She leaned in over the bar. "Tell me about him."

"Don't know much," the bartender admitted. "Just that his name's Matt Shaffer. Boss flew him in from L.A., where he was head of security for Montgomery Enterprises."

There was no avoiding it, she thought darkly. She was going to have to talk to Matt. The thought left her cold. "Do you know where I can find him right now?"

Kevin glanced at his watch. "He should be in his office. On the second floor, toward the rear." He gave her the numbers of the rooms where the monitors that kept watch over the casino guests as they tried their luck against the house were located.

Taking out a twenty, she placed it on the bar. "Thanks for your help."

Kevin slipped the bill into his vest pocket. "Any time, lovely lady," he called after her. "Any time."

She debated going up the stairs, then decided on the elevator. The car that took her up to the second floor was empty. Natalie stepped out of the elevator, looked around to get her bearings and then walked toward the rear of the floor.

"Into the Valley of Death rode the six hundred," she silently recited, digging deep for a line from a poem by Tennyson. Wrapping her hand around a brass handle, she opened one of the glass doors and walked in.

The woman whose desk was closest to the door looked up. "You can't come in here. This is a restricted area."

Natalie already had her ID in her hand and held it up. "I'm looking for Matt Shaffer," she told the woman.

God, even saying his name made her mouth go dry. She was supposed to be over him, to have moved on with her life. What happened?

The woman began to answer her. "He's—"

"Right here."

The deep voice came from behind her. Natalie felt every single nerve ending go on tactical alert at the same moment that all the hairs at the back of her neck stood up. Eight years had passed, but she would have recognized his voice anywhere.

* * * * *

*Why did Matt Shaffer leave
heiress-turned-cop Natalie Rothchild?
What does he know about
the death of Natalie's twin sister?
Come and meet these two reunited lovers
and learn the secrets of the Rothchild family in*
THE HEIRESS'S 2-WEEK AFFAIR
by USA TODAY *bestselling author*
Marie Ferrarella.
The first book in
Silhouette® Romantic Suspense's
wildly romantic new continuity,
LOVE IN 60 SECONDS!
Available April 2009.

CELEBRATE
60 YEARS
OF PURE READING PLEASURE
WITH **HARLEQUIN**®!

**Look for Silhouette®
Romantic Suspense in April!**

Love In 60 Seconds

Bright lights. Big city. Hearts in overdrive.

Silhouette® Romantic Suspense is celebrating
Harlequin's 60th Anniversary with six stories that
promise to bring readers the glitz of Las Vegas,
the danger of revenge, the mystery of a missing
diamond, and family scandals.

Look for the first title, *The Heiress's 2-Week Affair*
by *USA TODAY* **bestselling author
Marie Ferrarella, on sale in April!**

His 7-Day Fiancée by **Gail Barrett**	May
The 9-Month Bodyguard by **Cindy Dees**	June
Prince Charming for 1 Night by **Nina Bruhns**	July
Her 24-Hour Protector by **Loreth Anne White**	August
5 minutes to Marriage by **Carla Cassidy**	September

You're invited to join our Tell Harlequin Reader Panel!

By joining our new reader panel you will:

- Receive Harlequin® books—they are FREE and yours to keep with no obligation to purchase anything!
- Participate in fun online surveys
- Exchange opinions and ideas with women just like you
- Have a say in our new book ideas and help us publish the best in women's fiction

In addition, you will have a chance to win great prizes and receive special gifts!
See Web site for details. Some conditions apply.
Space is limited.

To join, visit us at
www.TellHarlequin.com.

THBPA0108

Silhouette

nocturne™ BITES

**Dark, sexy and not quite human.
Introducing a collection of
new paranormal short stories
by top Nocturne authors.**

Look for the first collection—

MIDNIGHT CRAVINGS

**Featuring Werewolf and Hellhound stories
from**

MICHELE HAUF, KAREN WHIDDON, LORI DEVOTI, ANNA LEONARD, VIVI ANNA and BONNIE VANAK.

**Indulge in Nocturne Bites
beginning in April 2009.**

Available wherever books are sold.

www.silhouettenocturne.com
www.paranormalromanceblog.wordpress.com

SNBITES09R

NEW YORK TIMES
BESTSELLING AUTHOR

CARLA NEGGERS

A red velvet bag holding
ten sparkling gems.

A woman who must
confront their legacy
of deceit, scandal and murder.

Rebecca Blackburn caught a glimpse of the famed
Jupiter Stones as a small child. Unaware of their
significance, she forgot about them—until a
seemingly innocent photograph reignites one man's
simmering desire for vengeance.

Rebecca turns to Jared Sloan, the love she lost to
tragedy and scandal, his own life changed forever
by the secrets buried deep in their two families.
Their relentless quest for the truth will dredge up
bitter memories...and they will stop at nothing to
expose a cold-blooded killer.

BETRAYALS

*Available February 24, 2009,
wherever books are sold!*

MIRA®

www.MIRABooks.com   MCN2623

Harlequin® Historical
Historical Romantic Adventure!

Undone!

THE RAKE'S INHERITED COURTESAN
Ann Lethbridge

Christopher Evernden has been
assigned the unfortunate task of minding
Parisian courtesan Sylvia Boisette.
When Syliva sets off to find her father,
Christopher has no choice but to follow
and finds her kidnapped by an Irishman.
Once rescued, they finally succumb to
the temptation that has been brewing
between them. But can they see past the
limitations such a love can bring?

Available April 2009
wherever books are sold.

www.eHarlequin.com

HH29541

REQUEST YOUR FREE BOOKS!

2 FREE NOVELS PLUS 2 FREE GIFTS!

Silhouette® Romantic

SUSPENSE

Sparked by Danger, Fueled by Passion!

YES! Please send me 2 FREE Silhouette® Romantic Suspense novels and my 2 FREE gifts (gifts are worth about $10). After receiving them, if I don't wish to receive any more books, I can return the shipping statement marked "cancel." If I don't cancel, I will receive 4 brand-new novels every month and be billed just $4.24 per book in the U.S. or $4.99 per book in Canada, plus 25¢ shipping and handling per book plus applicable taxes, if any*. That's a savings of at least 15% off the cover price! I understand that accepting the 2 free books and gifts places me under no obligation to buy anything. I can always return a shipment and cancel at any time. Even if I never buy another book from Silhouette, the two free books and gifts are mine to keep forever.

240 SDN EEX6 340 SDN EEYJ

Name _____ (PLEASE PRINT) _____

Address _____ Apt. # _____

City _____ State/Prov. _____ Zip/Postal Code _____

Signature (if under 18, a parent or guardian must sign)

Mail to the Silhouette Reader Service:
IN U.S.A.: P.O. Box 1867, Buffalo, NY 14240-1867
IN CANADA: P.O. Box 609, Fort Erie, Ontario L2A 5X3

Not valid to current subscribers of Silhouette Romantic Suspense books.

Want to try two free books from another line?
Call 1-800-873-8635 or visit www.morefreebooks.com.

* Terms and prices subject to change without notice. N.Y. residents add applicable sales tax. Canadian residents will be charged applicable provincial taxes and GST. Offer not valid in Quebec. This offer is limited to one order per household. All orders subject to approval. Credit or debit balances in a customer's account(s) may be offset by any other outstanding balance owed by or to the customer. Please allow 4 to 6 weeks for delivery. Offer available while quantities last.

Your Privacy: Silhouette is committed to protecting your privacy. Our Privacy Policy is available online at www.eHarlequin.com or upon request from the Reader Service. From time to time we make our lists of customers available to reputable third parties who may have a product or service of interest to you. If you would prefer we not share your name and address, please check here. ☐

SRS08R

HARLEQUIN®

INTRIGUE

B.J. DANIELS

FIVE BROTHERS

ONE MARRIAGE-PACT
RACE TO THE HITCHING POST

WHITEHORSE
MONTANA
The Corbetts

SHOTGUN BRIDE

Available April 2009

Catch all five adventures in
this new exciting miniseries
from B.J. Daniels!

www.eHarlequin.com

HI69392

Silhouette®
Romantic
SUSPENSE

COMING NEXT MONTH

Available March 31, 2009

#1555 PROTECTOR OF ONE—Rachel Lee
Conard County: The Next Generation
When Kerry Tomlinson has visions of a local murder, she turns to the police and retired DCI agent Adrian Goddard. He doesn't want to get involved, but his sense of duty compels him to protect her when someone finds out she's helping the police. As the killers draw closer, Kerry and Adrian must confront their own issues if they want to save each other.

#1556 THE HEIRESS'S 2-WEEK AFFAIR—Marie Ferrarella
Love in 60 Seconds
Her twin sister murdered, a priceless diamond ring missing and her former lover, Matt Shaffer, back in town—Las Vegas detective Natalie Rothchild's world has come unraveled. And now she must work with Matt in the face of danger to find her sister's killer and discover whether her heart can open to him again.

#1557 THE PERFECT SOLDIER—Karen Whiddon
The Cordasic Legacy
Military spy Sebastian Cordasic returned from war a changed man. Assigned to protect country music superstar Jillian Everhart from terrorists, he never expected to feel emotions for her. But when Jillian is taken by the same men who tortured him, Sebastian must face his past to rescue the woman he now can't live without.

#1558 IN SAFE HANDS—Linda Conrad
The Safekeepers
On a mission to find relatives of the orphaned baby she wants to adopt, Maggie Ryan locates the uncle, Colin Fairfax. But the drug lord who killed the child's parents finds Colin, too—and he wants him dead. Maggie and Colin join forces for protection, but they fail to protect their hearts against their growing attraction.

SRSCNMBPA0309